To my main hype-lady and first reader, Anya. Thank you for being you!

Lingering Shadows

LINGERING SHADOWS

Kate Aukes

Lingering Shadows

PROLOGUE

Rural Coalwick, IA – 1999

Sully swallowed hard, a lump rising in his throat as he stared down at the third letter he'd received that week.

That thieving bitch is dead. You're next.

The letters lacked a return address and signature and were never longer than a sentence or two. They said enough, though. Sully's hands shook as he folded the paper and shoved it in his pocket, closing the mailbox. He turned at the sound of a car passing to see a black sedan roll slowly by. The driver's window was down, and a man sat behind the wheel, intently watching Sully. Sully couldn't see the man's face, which was hidden behind a neck gaiter and sunglasses. However, the man's arm rested on the sill, his hand exposed and pinching a cigarette. There was a word tattooed near the webbing of his hand, but Sully couldn't read it from where he stood. He could only make out an ornate 'J' over the man's thumb.

Sully turned and jogged into the house as the car peeled off. On his way to his bedroom, he shouted up the stairs to his daughter.

"Carlie, grab your coat and come downstairs!" He could hear her footsteps as she moved into action above him. His other daughter, Lucia, sat immobile on the couch. She looked up at Sully, unable to act as she was bandaged head to toe on her left side. The week prior, a car crash had killed his wife and left his child suffering from numerous broken bones and extreme pain. They made eye contact as he passed, and she looked concerned.

In the bedroom, Sully squatted in front of the open closet door. Reaching into the corner, he peeled back the carpet to reveal a cut-out square in the floor, concealed by plywood. Sully removed the board, where a small safe sat. He punched in the code and yanked the door open. Stacks of money took up much of the space in the safe, and Sully grabbed a handful. He stuffed the bills in his pocket and retrieved a pistol that had also resided in the safe. Checking the chamber, Sully stuffed a handful of ammunition in his pocket and dropped the letter into the safe before closing and covering it once again.

Carlie was making her way down the stairs when Sully left the bedroom. He grabbed Lucia's coat and slippers from their place by the door and told Carlie to get her shoes on as he began dressing Lucia. Carlie obeyed without question. Sully scooped up Lucia from the couch and ushered Carlie out the door before following her, pulling the door closed behind him.

As they approached the truck, Lucia squirmed. Her breath came in ragged gasps, and she whimpered quietly. Upon opening the door and trying to place her inside, she lost her composure. She began screaming and crying, begging not to go. Still in a panic, Sully shook her and shouted, "Just get in the fucking car. We don't have time for this!"

Lucia flinched and went quiet, still breathing heavily and crying. She whimpered as he buckled her into her seat and shut the door. He bolted around the front of the truck to the driver's seat. He turned to look at the girls as he put the truck in drive and sped out of the driveway.

1

I stood frozen in place, my feet unable to move as if encased in concrete. I stood in a ditch next to a dead pine tree that was barely taller than my own five-foot-seven frame. My face grew tight as intense heat extracted every bit of moisture from my skin. I locked my eyes on an enormous mass of light just feet from me, as it bathed the ground and sky surrounding the brightest area in an undulating, tangerine glow. A massive tower of fire extended from the left side of the oblong ball of flames, and the sound of static filled my ears at a maddening volume. Suddenly the air felt thinner, and what oxygen I managed to pull into my lungs was white hot. My eyes teared as I gasped, breaking my paralysis and doubling over. I clawed at the collar of my tattered sweater, coughing and gagging on the thick, smoke-filled air, desperate to ease my breathlessness. I squeezed my eyes shut and shook my head violently. The static that filled my head abruptly stopped, and the sense that I wasn't alone overwhelmed me, as deafening silence filled the air. Turning my head slowly, I felt as though I might be sick. Before I could face whatever might be behind me, it threw me to the ground. I felt as though I'd been on the receiving end of a batter's swing to the center of my spine, but oddly enough, there was no pain; only all-encompassing fear. I began to raise my face from the ground as a familiar, yet warped voice hissed at me.

"Lucia, how could you?" The voice grew in volume as it repeated itself over and over again. I screamed and squeezed my eyes

shut, once again doubling over as the unseen entity continued to roar, "Lucia... Lucia... LUCIA!".

"Lucia, hey." My eyes snapped open, and I was immediately aware of the tears running down my face. I wiped at my eyes with the sleeve of my sweatshirt and cleared my throat as I picked my head up from the desk in front of me. As I returned to reality, I realized I was staring at an empty lecture hall. I had drifted off in class again and turned to look at who had rescued me from my public nightmare. A small, mousy girl patted my arm gently with a hand nearly covered by her pastel sweatshirt sleeve. She sat to my right, her dark hair framing her face as she displayed genuine concern. She fidgeted with her hands, picking at the corners of her fingernails, while waiting for me to come around. She swiveled carefully back and forth in her chair as she spoke again, "Are you alright? I've noticed you dozing in class a couple times, and if there's anything I can do to help, I'd be—"

"I'm okay, I promise." I cut her off, equal parts embarrassed, exhausted, and still shaken from the vivid scene I'd found myself in just moments before. "Thank you," I spit out as I stood to make a beeline for the door. I gathered my things hastily, my chair banging against the desk behind me as I left it behind, and I was still fumbling with my bag, papers dropping from it as I approached the door. As I crossed the threshold, I turned again to the girl without missing a beat, muttering a shaky "I'm sorry" and another "Thank you" before disappearing into the hallway.

I rounded the corner out of the lecture hall and picked up speed as I once again felt short of breath, as though my throat was closing. Tears threatened to return, and I blinked my eyes a few times to fight them off before throwing my hands up to my face and continuing my frantic power-walk down the never-ending gray hallway toward the nearest exit. I dropped my hands and glued my eyes to the floor. I became increasingly aware that all eyes from the straggling students were fixed on me. Six guys dressed in football uniforms had congregated in the hallway in a small alcove with several vinyl-covered armchairs. They fell silent as I passed, and I could feel their eyes sear into me as I made my way closer to freedom.

I finally reached the door and pushed my way through with more force than necessary, stumbling into the parking lot and breaking into a run once I had regained my balance. I felt as though I had never been so glad to see my powder-blue Taurus in my life. I flopped into the driver's seat and pressed the door lock before exhaling a sigh of relief, heaving my backpack into the back seat, throwing the car into gear and tearing out of the lot. Ironically, my eyes became dry as I merged onto the highway, seeming to have run out of tears.

###

I arrived at my small two-bedroom apartment after zoning out for the nearly half-hour drive. I parked and put both hands back on the steering wheel, gazing straight ahead at the fading purple wreath on my front door. I stayed that way for several minutes before snapping back to attention and exiting the vehicle. I began the short walk to my door without locking the car, mindlessly shuffling across the eroding pavement that lined the walkways and separated the grass from the narrow parking lot. As I walked, my sneaker caught a missing chunk of cement and I lurched forward, arms flailing. I managed to catch myself on one of the wooden pillars supporting the upstairs balcony. I rested my forehead against the chipping, beige paint, breathing a sigh of relief in gratitude that I hadn't hit the ground. I imagined that would have been a show all of Orestin would've loved to see. Since my father had dragged me here nearly thirteen years ago, far away from everyone and everything I ever knew, I had held on to the bitterness that kept me isolated for so long.

I unlocked the front door and stepped inside my apartment, entering into the living room. I stepped to the right and flipped on one of the two floor lamps flanking a long, low wooden table. The apartment building I lived in was affordable but outdated. Scanning the small room, my eyes scanned over the drab features: the low ceiling that lacked any lights, the sandy brown shag carpeting, the ugly brown pressboard doors that covered every closet and were each adorned with a myriad of large white scuffs. Worst of all were the walls; stark white and chunky in places from years of 'landlord-special' repairs. I had once found a massive wolf spider that had been squashed and then painted over. The low price and under-the-table 'lease' more than made up for the areas where convenience and beauty lacked. I'd only been seventeen when I moved in, or I likely would have had a bit more leverage to make cosmetic demands.

The familiar, acrid smell of urine suddenly assaulted my nose. "Damn dog," I muttered lowly, shuffling to the master bedroom doorway, where I saw my four-month-old Chinese Crested puppy, Sasha, lying belly-up in a sunbeam next to the sliding glass patio door. I rolled my eyes and snickered, my frown just barely lifting. "Warming your nips again, huh, Sash?"

Sasha either ignored me or didn't hear, and let out a long snore. I figured I'd better find the place where Sasha had popped a squat sooner, rather than later. I turned and padded down the hallway, eyes scanning the carpet for dark spots. My opportunity to follow the smell had long-since passed as the unseasonably high Tennessee heat had turned my poorly air-conditioned apartment into a hotbox of piss. Finding nothing, I returned to the living room and walked careful laps through the room. Still, I found the carpet devoid of wet spots or other waste. I sighed and put my hands on my hips, shifting my weight to one leg and furrowing my brow. "Oh my god, I'm a dumbass," I huffed as I turned back toward the hallway, realizing I hadn't actually been in either of the bedrooms. I'd poked my head earlier into both the kitchen and bathroom, which were laminate-floored and too small to do more than stand in. Neither contained any puddles, so I'd moved on immediately.

Rounding the corner into the master first, I gasped loudly as my foot met with an ice-cold, sopping-wet patch of carpet just past the threshold. My mouth remained ajar as I looked down and saw yellow liquid spread up the edges of my once white sock. The stench became impossibly stronger as uncomfortable moisture collected between my toes.

My gasp had broken Sasha from her slumber, and she popped up, the tags on her tiny, lime-green collar clanking together as she shook the sleep off. Sasha began her signature high-pitched groan, happily wiggling and bouncing her way across the room to my feet. I smirked and cracked a small smile. "You know, you're way too ugly to be so cute." Sasha continued groaning and stretched up onto her hind legs, placing her front feet on my knee as I spoke. "You're damn lucky you are, though!" I chuckled and reached down to stroke the puppy's small head, which was adorned by a patchy mane of long, white hair that extended down around her neck and up across the crests of her too-large ears. The same white hair covered all four paws and the underside of her tail, while the rest of her body comprised of soft, bald, peachy skin with the occasional brown patch.

Sasha retreated, and I bent my foot upward, removing my wet toes from the floor with an audible squish. I reached to my right to grab a hand towel from my bed. That morning, I had started to fold the clean laundry that had been sitting in the basket for more than a week. I praised my talent for procrastination as I tossed the cloth to the floor, marking the wet spot. Then I began the short trek to the bathroom, hobbling awkwardly on my heel down the hallway to clean myself up before returning to the bedroom to sanitize the carpet... again.

###

I sat cross-legged on the couch with my laptop open, a blank email to my statistics professor waiting on the screen. The cursor blinked at me, growing faster as I chewed on the corner of my pinky-nail in thought. Tightness growing in my gut, I wrote:

Dr. Lancaster,

I apologize for my falling asleep during the lecture this morning. I haven't been feeling well, and as a result haven't been sleeping well either. I wanted to reach out in hopes that you'd be willing to help me get caught up with today's lesson. I am happy to do any readings and/or extra assignments as necessary. I greatly appreciate any assistance you're able to provide in this matter.

Thank you,

Lucia Pierce

Lingering Shadows

After several typos and one massive cramp, I hit 'send', flipped my laptop closed, and looked down at my left hand. A long, fat, white scar extended nearly four inches down the length of my arm from the heel of my hand, dotted by old suture marks on both sides. I often mindlessly traced my thumb over the scar, which stood out against my olive skin. I rubbed my palm with the thumb of my other hand to relieve the cramp and extended my fingers as far as they would go. My index and middle finger opened nearly as far as they should, however, the other two fingers remained bent at almost a ninety-degree angle, unable to straighten any more. I gently used my right hand to force those two fingers to open more, stretching out the tight muscles. I winced as I did so, before rubbing my palm once more, opening and closing my hand a few times.

I glanced down at Sasha, who was curled up next to me, snoring. Carefully standing, I headed for my bedroom to change. I stepped around the towel on the still-damp floor and opened my dresser, opting for a gray camisole and black running shorts. I returned to the couch, stopping by the kitchen on my way for a glass of water. I grabbed a blanket from the ottoman and sat down, covering my lap. Sasha stirred and lifted her head. Upon noticing my return, she stood and stretched before climbing into my lap to curl up once again.

I pulled my cell phone from the waistband of my shorts and flipped it open, dialing my mom's number. Placing the speaker to my ear and letting my head fall back to rest on top of the cushions, I listened to Mom's voicemail box play, "You're reached Viv! Sorry I missed ya' but leave me a name and number and I'll getcha' called back as soon as I can!" The line beeped and I pressed 'call' again, listening to Mom's voice and imagining that she would one day answer the phone again. I did this often, especially in the quiet of the evening, when I remembered how alone I had become. All I wanted was my mom, but because of my stupidity, all I could have was a voicemail. It would never be enough.

Red and blue lights flashed from all directions as I stared at the sky. Screaming sirens pierced my ears, and my eyes fluttered as I wavered in and out of consciousness. The ground was frigid and unforgiving beneath me, causing me to shiver uncontrollably from a mixture of cold and terror. I dropped my head to the side and first became aware of the mess that was my long, black hair spread out around my shoulders. The sensation of a small object in my left palm soon captured my attention. My wrist bent sideways at a horribly unnatural angle, fibrous ropes of tendon snaking out from a long, ragged tear in my skin. I felt no pain, but my chest heaved as I focused my eyes on the item grasped tightly in my hand. My fingers gripped around a small claw clip, with clumps of hair and flesh jutting from between the plastic teeth. The clip glistened against the lights with a dark, sticky liquid. The heavy stench of iron hung in the air as the clip came alive in my hand, pulsating grotesquely. Blood gushed from the plastic, still clenched in my fist. The warm fluid covered my arm, seeping into my wound. I gagged, turning away and squeezing my eyes shut as hot tears flowed down the sides of my face and into my ears. I opened my mouth to scream, but only a quiet gurgle escaped, my jaw trembling as I began to choke. As my vision faded, I could hear what sounded like a woman moaning in pain. The sirens and the blood rushing in my ears muffled the sound as I struggled for breath and the surrounding scene disappeared.

I woke with a start, still sitting upright on the couch. Sasha had long since left my lap and gone to her bed near the TV stand across the room. My cell phone still clung to my ear, sticky and moist with sweat and tears. I peeled the phone away from my head, snapped it closed, and tossed it onto the side table where it landed with a loud, metallic *thunk* against the base of the lamp. I unfolded my legs, massaging my left thigh, where another very large scar ran down the length of the skin between my groin and knee. I dropped my feet to the floor and leaned forward, resting my head in my hands from the support of my elbows on my knees. I stayed that way for a while before rubbing at my tear-stained cheeks with my hands and drawing a shaky breath. I sat back and scooted down to the center of the couch, lying down fully and pulling my blanket up to my chin. I lay awake for more than an hour, staring at the wall across from me and replaying my haunting nightmare until I fell back into a fitful sleep.

2

I replaced a fallen earbud and resumed folding, piling towel upon towel onto my wire linen cart, *Ten Thousand Words* by The Avett Brothers filling my ears. I had spent the past four years as a laundry attendant at Fairview General Hospital, and admittedly, it was a lonely job. I appreciated the isolation, but never worked a shift without my iPod. Music kept the hours moving and shielded me from the bumps and groans of the basement laundry room. I finished my stack and turned to the mile-high pile of sheets that still awaited my attention. I rolled my eyes and sighed as I shuffled back over to the table where I spent most of my time. Just then, my song ended, and I reached into the pocket of my brown scrub pants to retrieve my iPod and find a new one. I shuffled through a few songs, noting nothing on my playlist making the cut until I heard the familiar intro to *Yet Again* by Grizzly Bear. I slipped the small, blue rectangle back into my pocket and bobbed my head lightly as I picked up the first quickly wrinkling sheet.

When every fitted sheet had been painstakingly folded, I gathered them onto the cart in the final available space before unfurling the blue-plastic cover that would encase the cart. I zipped it up and paused my music, winding up the headphones and placing the entire bundle into my pocket. I'd have loved to keep them in and block out the people I would inevitably pass on my way upstairs, but the administrator had been very clear that headphones, cell phones, and other electronic devices were not to be out while on the floors. I closed my eyes and took a breath before steering the cart out of the laundry room and into the hallway. Stopping just outside the door and doubling back, I grabbed a large, yellow rolling trash can: 'soiled barrels', as management liked to call them. Pulling it behind me, I retrieved the linen cart and continued to the elevator.

Floor two occupied the entire second story of the hospital, due to the nature of some of the patients it housed. I exited the elevator and stopped at a large set of double doors, which required a code to enter. I punched in the code and stood back as the doors opened slowly to allow me to pass into the unit, under a large, gray sign that read *2-PSYCH*. The doors closed more quickly than they had opened, and I continued down the sterile hallway to the nurses' station. I was met along the way with uncomfortable stares from patients and the occasional 'hello', which I responded to with a small smile and brief nod as I passed. At the nurses' station, Kayla Allen bounced around the corner, seeming to walk entirely on the balls of her feet. Her bright-pink *Hello Kitty* scrubs were a stark contrast to my own and revealed Kayla's outgoing nature.

"Hey Lulu! Linen time already?" Kayla chirped happily. I gritted my teeth at the nickname every time, but had decided to let it slide, as Kayla was one of the few coworkers I had come to accept as an acquaintance. Many of the nurses had taken to interacting with me somewhat dismissively when I made my rounds. Granted, I was content to keep to myself, but still somehow found the lack of acknowledgement a bit disappointing. Kayla had been the only floor staff to seem genuinely happy to see me. As much as I struggled to meet Kayla's energy, I was appreciative of it, and did my best to engage in return.

"Hi Kayla. How's your day going?" I met Kayla's eyes briefly before glancing back to my cart, then down the hallway, before returning to Kayla's face.

"Not too shabby, so far! Only one IM Ativan and we're already two hours into the shift! We normally have to have someone up here drawing up syringes of sedatives around the clock. I'm going for a record." Kayla laughed, and I lifted the corner of my mouth in a weak smirk. Kayla's expression changed, becoming almost concerned as she stepped into the utility room to retrieve a yellow barrel identical to the one I'd brought up. This one, however, was filled to the brim with towels and linens that I could already tell were filthy. "You okay? You seem more tired today."

"Uh..." I stuttered the beginning of a not-totally true response but was interrupted by the sound of a bed alarm down the hall. Relief washed over me as Kayla turned to face the direction the sound had come from.

"Oop! You're off the hook this time, but I'm watching you!" Kayla called back at me as she took off down the hall, blonde ponytail swinging behind her.

Now truly exhausted, and ready for a break from socialization, I traded barrels and retreated toward the elevator. As the doors rolled open, the sound of clattering metal and shouting suddenly filled the hallway. I stepped back toward the unit doors and peered through one of the small glass panels above the handles. About three-quarters of the way down the hallway, the floor was littered with napkins, pill cups, and plastic spoons, among other items from the nurses' cart. Seconds later, more miscellaneous items joined the pile. My eyes widened as I punched in my door code without looking and jogged down the hall toward the ongoing commotion, to find Kayla standing in the doorway of a patient room opposite a middle-aged woman.

The patient had light brown, shoulder-length hair and a stocky build. Her most notable feature at first glance was a large, caved-in portion of her head which began above her right eye and seemed to extend to her right ear. The eye itself looked to be intact but lolled out to the side as if unable to match the other. The woman was shouting incoherently but became completely silent as soon as she noticed me standing at the door. The woman's good eye widened, and she held my gaze for several moments.

"Lucia, help me out!" Kayla's voice broke me from my daze and back into action. Kayla had already approached the patient and placed both arms around one of hers. I mirrored the move exactly, and

Kayla freed one hand long enough to press a panic button on her badge reel. The woman's face grew impossibly red, veins in her forehead popping out as she thrashed against our hold and howled obscenities. Several sets of footsteps soon came into earshot, pounding down the hall as the woman seemingly grew in force tossed me, still hanging on for dear life, into an desk near the window. Pens and writing tablets clattered to the floor surrounded by a flurry of letters and photos. One particular photo of a towheaded young child and a middle-aged man caught my eye. My attention to the snap was short-lived as two more nurses entered the room in a frenzy. They were quick to help secure the situation further; one producing a syringe and plunging it into the woman's shoulder.

The woman screeched and continued whipping her body around. "Fucking bitch! Fucking bitch! You'll die! Fucking bitch!" Within minutes, the yelling quieted down, and it became much easier to hold the woman still. A few more minutes passed, and the nurses were able to lay her down in bed — fast asleep.

My heart pounded hard against my ribs. Kayla wiped her brow and blew air out of her mouth, placing her hands on her hips and looking over at me. "Make that two."

I stared at her, confused. "Huh?"

Kayla grinned. "Two IM Ativans." She started toward the hallway and gestured for me to follow. "Come on."

I gladly obeyed and left the room close on Kayla's heels. "What was that? Does she do that often?"

Kayla smiled and placed a hand on my shoulder. "Not usually quite that badly, but yes." Despite her smile, her eyes held a knowing sadness. "Brain injuries can really wreak havoc on a person."

I glanced back toward the room, my heart hurting for the woman as I read the name plate next to her door–*Jeannette Goodman*. "What happened to her?"

Kayla turned and bent down, scooping up plasticware and napkins by the handful. "It's an awful story, really. I guess her husband got her wrapped up in some shit with the law. Long story short, they apparently ended up trying to break into somebody's house a couple years ago and the homeowner shot at them. Managed to hit her right in the face, but the husband didn't get a scratch." She rose and stepped to the wall, where a mid-sized gray trash can stood. Dumping her armful of garbage and pulling it closer to the mess, Kayla squatted back down and continued clearing the floor.

I joined in as I listened, my jaw slack in disgust. We continued picking up for several minutes before I broke the silence. "Does he ever visit her? Is he even allowed?"

Kayla shook her head. "No. And no. They caught his ass on the front lawn and he's been locked up since. Besides, he'd be blocked from coming up here based on his offense." She paused, looking a bit puzzled. "I mean, I guess if he hadn't been caught we wouldn't really know, but it'd be pretty tough not to find out in this kind of case."

We finished the floor and stood, both emptying our last handful of trash into the can. Kayla picked it up and carried it down the hallway as we made our way back toward the nurses' station. At that point, I was dying to get back to my secluded 'office'. I took a step toward the end of the hall and forced a polite smile. "Well, I'd better get back. I'll see ya Monday?"

Kayla plopped down in the single rolling chair behind the L-shaped desk. "Alrighty. Yep, I'm here all next week! And then some, probably. Thanks for helping me out back there. You're a saint!" I rolled my eyes and turned, breathing a sigh of relief as I made my way back to the doors.

I returned to the laundry room, stopping in the entryway to deposit the contents of the new barrel into the last of a train of large, plastic bins that lined the wall next to the door. They often reminded me of dumpsters, which, due to the smell of used linens from all areas of the hospital, I wished at times were where I could take them. The stream of laundry coming down was never-ending, with all but one of the seven dumpsters sitting beneath a chute that connected to a different floor or department. Floor two was thankfully the only clinical floor I had to make rounds to, as being a psychiatric floor prevented a chute from being installed, for obvious safety reasons. I removed the lid of the barrel and pulled out the large, clear-plastic bag containing the soiled laundry. I hoisted it over the side of the dumpster and pinched the opposite end, dumping the contents inside. I recoiled as the abrasive stench of various bodily fluids and fecal matter ambushed my nose, wafting up in a warm, heavy wave as the pile of linens made contact with the bottom of the dumpster.

I took out my iPod, unraveling the headphones and popping them back into my ears. I hit 'play', then 'rewind' twice to hear Grizzly Bear once more. I chewed the inside of my bottom lip, pulling on a pair of latex gloves and tugging the first dumpster from the wall. I rolled it over to the single window opposite the doorway and began shoveling linens into the massive washing machine.

By the time I had gotten the front door open, I had already begun removing my shoes. I tossed them aside and peeled off my scrubs as soon as the door had closed, dropping them in a heap on the floor and heading to my bedroom in just my bra and underwear. I changed quickly into my shorts and tank top and flicked off the lamp next to my bed. I had still neglected to put away the laundry, and I shoved the pile to the corner of the bed as I crawled in. Much to my surprise, it took very little time to begin drifting off. Sleep didn't last long, though. The sound of Sasha's nails tapping on the bedframe and her high-pitched whine pulled me from my slumber. I yawned and blinked away the sleep, clicking the lamp back on and squinting down at Sasha, as a new realization hit me. "Shit, Sash. I'm sorry." I hopped out of bed and threw on a pair of sweatpants over my shorts. I snatched Sasha's leash off the dresser and clipped it to her collar. "We haven't been out!"

Feeling like a grade-A asshole, I unlocked the sliding-glass door and stepped onto the patio. Sasha bolted from the door and began rolling in the grass, wrapping her retractable leash several times around her bald little body. I snorted and shook my head as Sasha stood, shaking wildly. Sasha bounded over to me, and I untangled her from the leash, sighing. "Potty, Sasha!" Sasha turned-tail and pranced back into the grass, sniffing around and walking small laps. Finally, she found an acceptable spot and assumed the position. Once she had finished her business, Sasha trotted back to the patio, and I opened the door for her to re-enter the apartment. She did, and I released her from the leash, picked her up, and plopped her onto the bed. Sasha looked around for a moment before settling on a spot to sleep; right in the center of my clean laundry. *Fair enough,* I thought, rolling my eyes. I climbed back into bed and again turned off the lamp.

I stood still, my feet glued to the grass beneath me as intense heat scorched my skin. I opened my eyes slowly, immediately noting a huge wall of fire stretching into the sky just in front of me. Between the flickering orange and blue flames, I could just make out a tire flanked by lightly colored metal. Suddenly, a soft, loving voice called to me across the breeze. I immediately recognized it as the voice I only heard on tape. Mom! I opened my mouth to shout but found that no sound could escape.

The voice cried out pitifully, tormented. "Lucia, please..."

The rest of the statement was cut off by the same warped voice I had heard many times before. "You did this... YOU did this to her! WHY?" The voice turned into a horrifying scream as it began circling me, pulling the flames behind it and creating a tornado of fire that engulfed me. I covered my ears and squeezed my eyes shut, unable to muffle the impossibly loud screeching. My breathing became shallow as the air became too hot to inhale. Choking, I trembled with panic, desperately wishing for quiet and air. As quickly as it had begun, the screaming stopped. My eyes snapped open and found the sky dark, the air quiet. Once again, I was entirely alone. Almost entirely. The flames had left behind a blackened heap of metal, light puffs of smoke rising from the pile. I tested my feet again, this time to find them unstuck as I stepped cautiously toward the wreckage of a burned-out sedan, now illuminated by a single streetlight. Massive bubbles of silver paint hung from the doors, melted away by the heat of the blaze to reveal dull, gray plastic. As I drew closer, my gaze shifted to the inside of the car.

Nearly all of the windows had been smashed out, the charred interior of the vehicle glowing under a blanket of dying embers. As I peered into the car, taking in the scene before me, movement caught my eye.

A light, arrhythmic tapping sounded from the door opposite me. My heart leapt as four badly burned fingers crept over the base of the window frame. They gripped the plastic tightly, exposed ropes of muscle in motion to drag more of an arm into view. Blackened, hard skin sloughed off in sheets, uncovering the horribly dried out tissue beneath. My vision blurred just as a mess of tangled, brown hair emerged over the edge of the window.

I stirred and looked around the room, relieved to find that it had just been another nightmare. My gaze landed on my alarm clock. The bright-blue font stared back at me; three-forty a.m. I rubbed my eyes and sat up at the side of the bed before reaching to turn on the lamp. I looked over at my dresser and moved to sit on the floor in front of it. I opened the bottom drawer and pushed aside a few pairs of old jeans to reveal the edge of a wide, flat wooden box. I lifted it from the drawer and set it in my lap, running my fingers over the smooth, dark finish. I opened the metal clasp at the front, revealing a small, pink photo album, a silver ring, and a few notes I'd received from kids in my fourth-grade class. My teacher, Mrs. Chapman, had assigned the class the task of making sympathy cards for me after Mom's death. They had been mailed to me in the hospital together in a giant manila envelope. Nurses had taken turns reading them to me, deciphering the unpolished handwriting as best they could. It had been equal parts endearing and embarrassing, but that no longer mattered. By the end of the year, my father, Sully, had moved me to Tennessee with my sister. I'd been dragged along, ripped away from everything familiar during the worst year of my life.

I reached into the box, taking the ring in my hand and running a thumb over it before placing it on my left index finger. The ring was an all-silver band made up of simple daisies chained together. It was nothing fancy, and far from an expensive ring, but it was Mom's favorite. She had worn her daisies for as long as I could remember. Over time, the silver had grayed, and the band was no longer as perfectly round as it had been. It had developed a slightly oval shape from Mom's many years of near-daily wear.

I grabbed the photo album next, flipping through various pictures of myself as a young child; birthday photos taken in the backyard with classmates I barely spoke to, candid shots of me enjoying the sights on one of many trips Mom had planned just for the two of us, the obligatory 'baby in the bathtub' snaps. I stopped at the back cover, on a photo that I had taped into the album when I ran out of space in the plastic sleeves. I turned the photo over without removing the tape and rotated the whole album to read what was written on the back. Scrawled in Mom's curly cursive hand was the last day of her life: *November 29th, 1999–Coalwick, IA.* I would turn nine the following day, and Mom had arranged for a road trip out to Colorado to celebrate. However, only I had returned home. We'd made it all the way to Colorado, and had gotten within two hours of Durango, where we planned to stay the first night. I'd been bored, as I often was as a child on long car trips, and I had been reading aloud from a book of jokes I had checked out from school. Mom laughed along as she drove, but at one point I had added in a more off-color joke I had learned on the bus. *Stupid*, I reminded myself. *You've always been so stupid!* Mom had turned to scold me and had lost control of the car. I went to the hospital and Mom went to the morgue. *Happy birthday, kid.*

I flipped the photo back over and turned the album back around. Mom and I smiled widely, standing between Dad's Chevy Silverado and Mom's silver Buick LeSabre. Mom had loved that car so much. She had saved for several years to buy a car, taking longer to reach her goal as she put much of her earnings toward spending time with 'her girlie'. She was a teacher's aide in Whitehill, so she didn't bring in much money anyway, but she was always happy to put what she had into being with me. The birthday trip in ninety-nine was no exception, and I had loved every moment that I had Mom to myself. Dad could be a demanding and sometimes mean man and had monopolized Mom's time outside of what she set aside for me. I studied Mom's face, soft and inviting. She smiled widely, and I thought back to how excited she had been for the trip. Her shoulder-length hair was tied up in the back, most likely in one of her countless claw clips, which she wore nearly every day. Dad had always bitched about finding them everywhere in the house, but I always giggled when I found one, clipping it to her dining chair in the entryway. It was a game of sorts, to see how many I could attach to the chair before she removed them. My record had been six. A teardrop fell onto the photo, landing on little Lucia's foot. Then another fell, and I wiped them away, before swiping the back of my hand across my face.

I laid a finger gently on Mom's face as I cried. "I'm so sorry." The words came out distorted, strangled by sobs as I closed the album and brought it to my chest. I clamped a hand over my mouth, muffling the cries as they escaped my body too violently to allow the air to be replaced in between.

I woke once again, roused by the sound of my phone's alarm ringing. I didn't remember having brought it to bed with me, much less to the floor in the middle of the night, but I fished around with my hand until I found it under the edge of the bed. I flipped it open and silenced the alarm, glancing at the date on the home screen; *Sunday, November 18th, 2012.* I closed the phone and set it back on the floor, staring up at the ceiling. I lay on the ground, the album still plastered to my chest. My ears were wet with tears, reminding me of the events of the night before. I sat up slowly and returned the album to its place inside the box before rearranging the drawer it had come from. I stood and looked at Sasha, still fast asleep on the bed. Though I didn't remember falling back to sleep, the nightmare that had shaken me awake in the dead of the night replayed in my mind. Desperate and at a loss for a way to relieve the pain, I looked down to my hand, where Mom's daisies rested peacefully around my finger. *Mom would tell me to go to church.*

Since Mom's death, I hadn't ever given much thought to my stance on religion, or God. Thinking of it at present, I still didn't know what to believe. However, I decided to visit the only church in town that I knew, hoping that God, or Mom, or someone would tell me how to go on. I patted my hands on the bed, waking Sasha, who stretched before prancing over to my waiting arms. I set Sasha on the floor and let her out into the backyard, then returned to the heap of laundry on the bed. I sifted through, looking for a decent outfit that hadn't become too wrinkly. I settled on a black turtleneck sweater with gray and black plaid slacks. I'd just worn them to a meeting at work; the first time they'd seen the light of day in quite a while. I dressed quickly, stepping in front of the dresser, which was topped with a large vanity mirror. I brushed away a bit of dog hair, and tucked in the sweater, adding a black belt and clasping the silver buckle as I walked to the patio door to let Sasha back in. She came flying through as soon as the it slid open, and I bent down to pet her. Sasha leaned into my hand and wiggled. I sighed and gave her mostly-bald head one last stroke before standing and heading for the door. I slipped into a pair of black flats, then grabbed my car keys and stepped outside.

I pulled up to Redeemer Road Evangelical Church just barely late, a habit I seemed to repeat everywhere I went. As I parked, I almost changed my mind and went home, feeling embarrassed by the thought of walking through a crowded group of strangers, especially late. I guessed if anywhere should be forgiving of my tardiness, it would be here.

The sanctuary was packed, as I'd expected. The floor creaked as I snuck into the back pew, thankful that most people seemed not to notice. Those that saw me didn't make a fuss, rather they just smiled politely and nodded in my direction before turning back around in their seats. I sat and halfheartedly listened to the sermon, given by an elderly woman with dark-rimmed glasses and too-long, too-white hair. The tone changed, grabbing my attention as the congregation began taking turns bringing up their 'joys and concerns'. Many people stood and talked about family members who had had babies, completed some kind of school, started new jobs, were sick and in the hospital, or worse. My eyes bounced around the room from person to person as they stood to speak. When the last person sat down, I looked down at my hands resting in my lap and picked at the chipping emerald-green paint on my nails.

The pastor called for any last announcements, and my eyes widened as a high-pitched, squeaky, familiar voice responded, "Just one! I'd like to say something, just real quick." I raised my head to see a short mop of blond hair tied half-up in a loose knot. The woman turned to scan the entire congregation as she stood to speak, and I knew the scrunched-up smirky smile well.

I gasped and spoke under my breath, so softly I almost couldn't hear myself. "Carlie?"

3

I stared, incredulous, as my sister addressed the packed room. "I have some news to share about my dad, Sully." Carlie swiveled slowly, trying to face everyone she could as she spoke. "I'd like to thank the congregation on behalf of my family, for all the prayers and well-wishes during Dad's illness. I'm sad to report that he went home to God on Wednesday." A wave of awe's washed across the room and Carlie nodded, still oscillating. I suddenly became very aware of how long it had been since I had last come to church. Carlie and Dad had apparently continued coming here after I had left home over five years prior. I could have chosen another church, but I hadn't given it much thought. Redeemer Road was the only church I had ever been to after coming to Tennessee and seemed like the most comfortable option, despite the now obvious chance of running into family.

Carlie finished speaking, and a few moments later, the closing prayer signaled the end of the service. Nearly everyone rose at once, some shuffling toward the exit immediately. Others milled around the sanctuary, greeting each other and sharing stories of their week. I stood to leave, making my way to the aisle, when I caught Carlie's eye. Carlie flashed me a brief, subtle look of surprise before scowling and pressing on toward the door with a small, copper-haired boy in tow. I followed, pushing through the crowd of people and through the doors to the parking lot. Carlie was hastily making her way to a gray sedan at the front of the lot.

"Carlie, wait!" I called after her.

Carlie turned to glance in my direction before opening the back door of the car and lifting the toddler into his car seat. "Stay here, baby. Mommy's gonna be just a minute. Then we'll go home and have some lunch!" The boy grinned and clapped his pudgy little hands. Carlie closed the car door and turned back to me. "What? Why are you here?"

I didn't answer, responding with a question of my own. "Why didn't you tell me Dad was sick? Or that he died?"

Carlie furrowed her brow, appearing frustrated. "Why would I?"

"Because he was my dad, too. I deserved to know." I swallowed the lump that began forming in my throat, blinking back tears.

"Oh, did you?" Carlie laughed. "You left! No contact, remember? You never called, never came around. Why should I have assumed you'd care?" Carlie cocked her head, stepping closer to me. Carlie was several inches shorter than me, but infinitely more confrontational. Even when we were children, where I might start something, Carlie was happy to engage and finish it. She was my half-sister, and I supposed she must have gotten her extra fire from her mother.

"I left because he..."

Carlie cut me off. "Was mean, I know," she mocked. "But he was never that way before your mother." She spit the last two words like venom, and they landed on their mark.

I winced, and the tears spilled over as I became furious. "What the hell is that supposed to mean? All she ever did was take care of him!"

"He was a happy man, Lucia. Never grumpy, never short. Happy. Then Viv came along and he changed. She had him stressed out beyond his limit. All the time! You never understood because you were so young, and she spent so much time doting on you." Carlie's face softened slightly. She looked tired, almost. She glanced back to the car, where her son had fallen asleep despite the argument unfolding just inches from him. "Look. I've gotta go. I'm over all this; I've moved on. You should too."

I opened my mouth to speak, but Carlie raised a hand to cut me off.

"I'm not continuing this conversation with you. I've gotta go. Bye, Lucia." She yanked open the driver's door of the car and dropped into the seat, closing the door behind her. The lock clicked as she put the car in drive and pulled away, leaving me to watch her go. I trudged across the lot to my car, keeping my eyes glued to the pavement all the while.

I plopped onto the couch and opened my laptop, which I had left on the Google homepage. In the search bar, I entered *Orestin, TN obituaries*. The first link took me to the obituary page for 'The Hawkeye Daily Register'. I scrolled through names and photos of lost loved ones, memorialized by grieving families left behind. It didn't take long for me to come across my father's picture. Dad's worn, tired face stared back at me from the screen, deep wrinkles from years of heavy sunlight exposure outlining his features. His once-brown hair had gone almost entirely gray, and his brown eyes had a dull appearance, as if the light had gone out of them entirely. He also appeared to have lost a lot of weight. Once somewhat chunky, Dad appeared gaunt and ghostly, and his eyes seemed sunken in, despite the smile painted on his face. I clicked on his photo and opened the full obituary, which was short and sweet:

Sullivan James Pierce, 55, joined his savior in heaven on Wednesday, November 15th 2012 at 4:15 a.m. After a five-year battle with lung cancer, he passed peacefully at Grand View Hospice Home, with his daughter and grandson by his side. Sullivan was born on March 18th, 1957 to Arthur and Lily Pierce in Shiah, North Carolina. He is preceded in death by his parents and by his wife, Sarah Vivian Barlowe. He is survived by his daughter Carlie Pierce, grandson, James Crofton, and brother, Gary Pierce, along with three nieces who all miss him dearly. He is being cared for by Raymond and Sons Mortuary in Orestin. Memorials in Sullivan's name can be directed to Grand View Hospice Home.

I closed the laptop and leaned my head back on the couch. I supposed maybe Carlie was right; I didn't deserve to know that Dad had died and didn't deserve to be included in his obituary. I had caused Mom's death and then abandoned Dad just a few years before his. I thought back to the day I left; how my father had tried and tried to get me to stay. His usually abrasive exterior had faltered, if only just a bit. I had been in such a hurry to leave that it had blinded me. *He must have been sick when I left. He must have known.* Guilt overwhelmed me. Dad had been grumpy, even a downright asshole at times, but did he deserve to be deserted?

I decided I could at least show up for his funeral. Carlie hadn't given details on services for him at church and hadn't included them in the obituary, so I opened my computer back up to search for the funeral home's contact. When I found it, I set the laptop next to me on the couch and stood, pacing the floor as I dialed. I steadied my breath as the line rang, waiting for someone to pick up.

An older-sounding woman answered the phone with a cheery tone. "Raymond and Sons, how may I help you?"

I hesitated for a moment before responding. "Uh, hi. This is Lucia Pierce. I just wanted to find out the times for Sullivan Pierce's memorial services. He was my dad."

The line was quiet. Finally, the woman's voice returned. "Oh, honey. Mr. Pierce won't be having any services. He specified in advance that he didn't want any kind of gathering, rather that an option to send a memorial to the hospice home be provided."

I looked down as my stomach sank. "Oh. Okay. Well, thanks anyway."

"You're welcome, hon... Oh wait! Lucia Pierce! I have a message here that was left for you. Your father's lawyer needs to get in touch with you, but he couldn't find a good number, so he called here hoping you'd be involved in arrangements. Something about assets in the will." Shuffling and clunking noises crowded the other end of the line, and I pulled the phone a little further from my ear. "Here, I'll get you the number so you can give him a call."

I raised an eyebrow and hurried to the kitchen for a pen and paper. I copied the phone number down, having been told to ask for a 'Mr. Vaughan'. "Thank you. I'll get him called right away." We exchanged polite goodbyes and I hung up the phone. I immediately dialed the number for the law offices as butterflies fluttered around in my stomach.

As I had expected on a Sunday afternoon, the outgoing voicemail greeted me. "Thank you for contacting Vaughan and Associates. Our hours are Monday through Friday, eight to four, and Saturday, eight to noon. We look forward to assisting you. Please leave your name and number along with a brief message, and one of our staff members will call you back as soon as possible."

I left my name and number to the empty line and stated that I was returning a call for Mr. Vaughan. I ended the call and tossed my phone onto the couch, looking down at my outfit. I was not fond of dressing up and found myself itchy; missing my jeans and Old Navy crewneck. I let out a breath that I didn't realize I had been holding and went to my bedroom to change. When I returned, my phone pinged to let me know I had received a text. I sat back down and flicked the phone open. The message had come from Andrea Miles, one of my night-shift coworkers at the hospital.

> ***<u>Andrea</u>: 'Hey! I'm on my way out of town for a family emergency. Could you cover for me tomorrow night?'***

I enjoyed covering shifts at work, purely for the distraction and extra money. I didn't get the opportunity as often as I would like, so I was eager to jump on shifts whenever they became available.

> ***<u>You</u>: 'Yep, no problem. 7:30, right? You'll take care of the schedule with Deb?'***

<u>Andrea</u>: 'Sure thing! And yes, 7:30. TYSM!'

I picked up my scrubs, which were still in a heap by the door, and tossed them in the hamper by my bed. *I guess it's laundry day, then.*

4

The sound of my phone ringing roused me from an oddly peaceful sleep. Morning light shone through the vertical blinds hanging across the patio door at the end of the bed. Rolling over to face my nightstand, I fumbled for my cell, grabbing it and flipping it open. I tugged the cord from the charging port, tossing it aside with a loud *click* as it hit the bedframe on the way to the ground. I put the speaker to my ear, brushing away tangled strands of hair that had welded themselves to my face overnight.

"Hello?" My voice was raspy and sounded terrible. I cringed as soon as the word left my mouth.

A man's voice came across the line. "Good morning, this is Wesley Vaughan. I'm looking for Lucia?"

I snapped to attention, all grogginess seeming to leave me at once as I cleared my throat and sat on the edge of the bed. "Yes, that's me. I was just returning a message yesterday that I got from the funeral home."

"Yes, of course. I'm glad you reached out! I have something I need to discuss with you in regard to your father's passing. I don't have much in the way of appointments today. Would you be able to stop by?"

My stomach tightened. "Um, sure. Where's your office?"

Mr. Vaughan gave me an address as I scrambled out of bed and into the kitchen to write it down. I thanked him and promised to be there before noon, though I hadn't ever looked at the clock to see if that was a promise I could keep. I checked the clock on my phone as I walked back into the bedroom. It was just past ten, and I would have plenty of time to get ready and make it across town.

###

Lightly stained wooden panels adorned the walls of the Vaughan and Associates office. I studied the dark-maroon carpeting below from one of the ten gray plastic chairs in the small waiting room, bouncing my leg anxiously. I'd never set foot in a law office before. I had never had a reason to. The air was incredibly stuffy, and I could feel the sweat beading on the back of my neck. A large, golden, sunburst-shaped clock ticked on the wall behind me. I looked up from the floor and reached back to tie my hair up in a messy knot at the back of my head.

A scrawny young man with bright-red hair and a thick spray of freckles stood from the front desk. "Lucia?"

He had butchered my name so badly that I may not have known to respond in a room full of people. But I was the only one in the waiting room and raised my hand awkwardly as I stood from my chair. The receptionist gestured for me to follow him and we set off down a short hallway behind his desk. He led me to an open door at the end of the hallway and waved me inside.

An elderly man with wire-rimmed glasses and thin, combed-over gray hair sat behind a massive desk. He smiled warmly and pointed to an armchair across from him as I entered. "Lucia! Have a seat. Thank you for coming down. I'm Wesley."

I nodded and sat down, sinking deep into the cushion. The chair was a black pleather, and cracks covered every inch, a sign that the chair had been a staple in the office for a very long time.

I readjusted to sit straighter while Wesley flipped through a long stack of files. He pulled a thin one from the stack and opened it.

"So, I wanted to meet with you to let you know what was left for you after Sullivan died." He adjusted his glasses and glanced up at me, confirming that I was paying attention. "It's a property in rural Coalwick, Iowa. If I'm not mistaken, I believe it was your family home for a while."

My jaw fell open in a mix of surprise and confusion. "That doesn't make any sense. My dad and I were never really very close."

Wesley turned back to the file as he clarified. "Well, it wasn't left by him, per se. It was left in trust for you by your mother. At the time of her death, you were too young to legally take possession of it so it stayed with Sullivan until what was supposed to be your eighteenth birthday. Given the break in your relationship and the fact that the key is still here, I'd imagine you weren't aware of that until now." I said nothing, just continued to stare. Wesley smiled and continued, "You've technically owned the property for going on four years. Happy early birthday, by the way."

I flashed a polite smile and nodded. "Thanks. What do I do with it? I mean, I've never owned land or a house, or anything like that. And why didn't my dad just sell the place after we left?"

"It wasn't his to sell. But believe me–he tried. Your mother was very particular in the terms of her will. If you ask me, it's a bit peculiar for someone who was only in her thirties at the time, especially someone who was not terminally ill." He removed a small silver key, closed the file, and looked back to me. "You can do whatever you'd like with it." Wesley stood and rounded the desk unsteadily, bracing himself with his free hand. I rose and extended a hand as Wesley passed me the key. "Call it a fresh start."

Wesley escorted me to the door and I made my way back down the hall and to the sidewalk outside. I looked down at the key Wesley had given me, turning it over in my hand. It was still shiny and seemed to have never been used, likely a copy made just for me. I reached into the pocket of my jeans to retrieve my keyring, adding the new key with some difficulty. My fingers cramped, and I stretched them as I continued to my car.

Lingering Shadows

The large hospital washing machines whirred, and I watched its contents spin around and around, all the while contemplating my conversation with Wesley that morning. I set about folding and stacking towels as Wesley's words played on repeat in my mind. 'Call it a fresh start,' he had said. I'd been looking for something different for years, but still I found myself uncertain of what to do with this newfound opportunity. I was afraid, maybe scared, to embark on yet another new adventure on my own. Yet I longed to go home so badly. I finished what I could and sat down at the folding station, fiddling with the tag on my scrub top as I waited for the next load to be ready, continuing to think. By the time the dryer buzzed, I had made up my mind.

I swapped the laundry before stepping into the hallway and headed toward the back door. Dozens of empty medical supply boxes sat unevenly piled atop one another on both sides of the door. I began the tedious task of breaking each box down, as night-shift laundry aides were tasked with anyway, setting a stack aside for myself. I dropped my backpack on top of the stack as a reminder to myself and bent down to take out a notebook and pencil. I returned to my table and wrote two notes. The first was my resignation, which was to be effective immediately. The second was a short note for Samuel Norton, a maintenance tech with whom I'd become almost friendly.

Hi Sam,

I need to ask a favor. Please call me when you get a chance.

Lucia

I finished the rest of my last shift at Fairview General Hospital the following morning. As I straightened up the laundry room to leave, I left my name badge and keys on the corner of the table. I then made my way to the hallway to collect my boxes and backpack, pausing for one final look at the room as I went.

###

I sat on the floor of my bedroom, piles of clothing scattered around me. A reconstructed box sat in front of me, filling up as I sorted through years of garments that hadn't been out of the closet in quite some time. Once I had stuffed the box, I crammed the flaps of the top closed and taped it shut. I labeled it *donate* and shoved it up against the wall with my legs. A jolt of pain shot up my left leg from knee to hip. I massaged my thigh with the heels of my hands, flexing my leg a few times. As the pain subsided, I sighed in annoyance and traced the length of the long red scar with my eyes from knee to groin, shaking my head.

The phone rang, pulling me from my thoughts. I flipped the phone open and accepted the call, grateful for the distraction. "Hello?"

"Hey, Lucia. It's Sam. I got your message at work. Everything okay?" Sam sounded concerned, and suddenly I wished I had given him more information in the note I left.

"Hi, Sam. Yeah, yeah, I'm all good. Just needing some help with something. I didn't mean to worry you."

His voice brightened a bit. "No worries! What's up?"

"So," I started, a knot forming in the pit of my stomach. I couldn't put my finger on why I was getting so nervous. "I'm moving, and I need a hand lifting the heavier things in my apartment. Would you be up for something like that?"

Sam was quiet for a moment. "Yeah, absolutely. Are you going far?"

"Yep. Iowa, actually." We talked about the house and how I'd gotten it, and agreed on November thirtieth as moving day. We hung up, and I switched gears to calling my landlord. I decided it would be best to just get the phone calls out of the way at once. Receiving no answer, I left a voicemail to notify the landlord of my plans to leave at the end of the month and asked for a call back.

###

November thirtieth arrived quickly, but I was ready. As the days since learning that I could go home passed by, my initial fears had turned to excitement. Winter break had begun for Evergreen Community College, and I had met with my advisor to discuss the process of transferring credits in the spring.

Looking around, I took in the shocking number of boxes that surrounded me, wondering how anyone with more square footage would ever move house, as just moving my small apartment was already proving to be an enormous task.

A knock on the door brought me back to attention. I checked the peephole and found Sam outside. Sam smiled as I opened the door. "Hey, Sam. Thanks for doing this."

Sam stepped inside. At six-foot-four, he towered over me, and I had to crane my neck to speak with him. He'd come prepared, carrying the toolbox I had often seen him with at the hospital, and wearing a back brace that fit snugly around his rounded belly. Sam noticed me looking at the brace and chuckled. "Like it? I never used to wear one, but in my old age I've taken to it after about the fourth time I threw my back out at work."

I smirked. "Forty-three isn't old, Sam."

Sam grinned and scanned the room. "If you say so." He cleared his throat and turned back to me. "Alrighty, then. What's first?" He set the toolbox on the floor next to the door and put his hands on his hips.

"Furniture, maybe? The U-Haul's out front."

We started with the larger furniture, hauling out my bed frame, mattress, and couch first. I had dismantled any piece of furniture I could and bundled the pieces into bags or stacks wrapped with masking tape. Piece by piece, the apartment emptied. Sasha bounced happily around the now huge-looking space, rolling and rubbing her face on the carpet. I watched her for a moment, before picking her up and strapping her into her harness, attaching her leash. I set Sasha back on the floor and walked with her through the apartment one more time to make sure I had accounted for everything. Satisfied, I set my keys on the kitchen counter and locked the doorknob. I pulled the door closed and led Sasha to the U-Haul truck, which had a tow dolly on the back that Sam had loaded my car onto.

Sam leaned against his truck and watched as I walked Sasha around to relieve herself before putting her into the cab of the truck. I had laid a jacket on the passenger seat for her to sit on, and she set to work nesting in it as soon as I put her down. I closed the door and walked around to the other side, where Sam now stood waiting.

"Thank you so much for your help, Sam." I said.

Sam nodded. "You're so welcome. What's the plan for when you get to Iowa? Unloading, and such."

I paused. I hadn't thought quite that far ahead. As much planning as I had done for leaving, I had forgotten the rest. "I'm not a hundred percent sure yet. I've got a little bit of money saved, so I'm leaning on that to at least get me into the house."

Sam nodded again, pursing his lips and patting me once on the back, harder than he likely realized. I stifled a gasp as some of the air left my body and Sam spoke once more, looking at his watch. "Almost eleven already. It's gonna get late on ya pretty quick if you don't get on the road soon. Drive safe, and don't be a stranger, okay?"

I chewed on my bottom lip and nodded, climbing up into the driver's seat of the U-Haul. I started the truck and pulled away, glancing up into the rearview mirror. Sam waved goodbye, his short, brown hair rustling as a cool wind picked up.

5

I pulled into the driveway of my childhood home, careful not to miss the gravel entrance in the dark. I was only able to see at all thanks to the full moon, which cast a dull blue light across the property. Ample trees and the large two-story farmhouse cast eerie shadows on the ground. The house stood tall, a black silhouette against the cloudless, star-filled sky. I parked the truck and leaned over to the passenger side, dropping the glove box open to retrieve a flashlight before scooping up Sasha, grabbing my backpack, and hopping out of the truck. Butterflies fluttered in my stomach as I approached the house, wading through knee-high grass and stopping only long enough to let Sasha do her business. The stairs creaked as I climbed onto the porch, placing the flashlight under my chin to free my hands. I took out my keys and fumbled for the right one. When I put the key in the lock, it turned easily as if it was already unlocked. The door groaned loudly as I stepped inside to total darkness. Dust floated like a snow flurry in the yellow ray of my flashlight, and the air around me smelled musty and stale.

I felt along the wall by the door for a light switch, hopeful that my memory would serve me well. It did, and the switch was exactly where I remembered. I flipped it, but nothing happened. I rolled my eyes, feeling stupid. *Makes sense.* I opted to wait for morning to look around further when the sun came up. I made my way upstairs, tripping on an upturned chair as I went. At the top of the stairs, I could make out the familiar shape of the short, narrow hallway. At the opposite end of the hall was my childhood bedroom, and when I stepped inside, a flood of memories rushed back to me. One in particular hit me like a ton of bricks as I looked at my small twin bed, still made up from the last night I'd slept there as a child. I remembered being woken up by Mom to leave for my birthday trip to Durango, exactly thirteen years prior. Mom had sat down on the edge of my bed and woken me gently by stroking my forehead with her palms as she had so many times before. I couldn't help but smile, as my throat tightened and eyes watered. After the accident, I'd had casts over most of the left side of my body–my femur crushed, and wrist mangled. Dad had made me sleep in the recliner from that point on, though it was just days before we had left the house in a rush. I had never thought I'd get to come home.

I walked over to the bed, peeling back the top cover to remove most of the dust that had collected. I ran a hand across the flannel covers and suddenly felt exhausted. I reached down and picked up Sasha, plopping her down onto the bed as well and releasing her from her harness. She shook her body fiercely, rearranging whatever hair she had until she was satisfied. I laid down and stared at the ceiling for a while, feeling almost like a child again, pretending to sleep and waiting for my mom to come wake me.

My eyes snapped open at the sound of distant knocking, audible only due to the deathly quiet of the otherwise empty house. I sat up, blinking my eyes to clear away the sleep. My stomach dropped when I could see clearly again. The room had been trashed. The closet had been emptied onto the floor with one sliding door torn off the track, and every drawer of the dresser was open and had been rifled through. The knocking paused as I stared on in shock. I stood and let Sasha down from the bed, shuffling over to the door and down the hall to the stairs. I hoped the other bedrooms weren't as turned over as mine, and wondered how mine had become that way in the first place.

Sadly, I found the living room in a similar state. The television was upside down on the floor and nearly all the furniture had been moved, leaving drag marks on the cream-colored carpet. Yet another closet had been gutted, its contents spread about the room. I found the chair I'd nearly fallen over the night before, which had come from the small dining set at the back corner of the entryway. Not a single picture hung correctly on the wall; some were wildly askew, while others were missing entirely and left vibrant patches on the otherwise faded green wallpaper. The knocking resumed, more rapid in pace, and I went to the picture window as I had done when I was a nosey little girl and someone was at the door. I peeked out from the very edge of the drawn-back curtain, just barely able to see the porch.

A young man dressed in ragged jeans and a maroon t-shirt paced the porch, his heavy work boots thumping with every step. He stopped, holding a cell phone to his ear with one hand and combing the other through his chin-length, toffee-colored hair. I couldn't make out what he was saying, but he was mid-sentence when he turned and spotted me. He smiled and gave a small wave, muttering something into the phone and hanging up before motioning for me to come to the door.

I dragged my fingers through my hair quickly and opened the door about halfway. The man continued smiling and turned to look toward the driveway, where a large, yellow tractor sat idling. He turned back to me and spoke. "Hi, I work in the field behind your house. I just wanted to stop by and let you know that our crew will be through once or twice a day during the spring and fall to get into the field." He paused for a moment and looked down at his feet. "And that I accidentally dug a rut in your driveway." I opened my mouth to say something, and he continued, "I'm Isaac, by the way. Isaac Young."

I lifted the corner of my mouth in a polite half-smile. "Lucia Pierce. You guys can use the driveway as much as you need to. I'll keep it clear."

"When did you move in? We always thought this place was abandoned." Isaac examined the front of the house, and I stepped onto the porch to do the same. The house certainly looked abandoned, as it had been. The once-white siding looked gray with dirt and the roof was missing a portion of its shingles, many of which lay scattered in the overgrown front yard. Old, green shutters clung to each window, most of them in decent shape while a couple hung on by just one hinge. All were covered in bald spots from years of chipping paint.

"It was. I just got here late last night. My family lived here when I was a kid, but my dad moved us when I was nine. He passed a little while ago and the house was left to me." I kicked at a piece of shingle with a socked foot, wringing my hands nervously.

Isaac crossed his arms and sighed. "I'm sorry to hear about your dad. Do you think you'll stick around?"

"I hope so, but I wasn't really expecting the mess that's here. It's gonna take me forever to get it cleaned up," I sighed.

Isaac smiled again, reaching up to scratch his arm. He had big, soft, brown eyes, so dark it was difficult to make out where his pupils were, and when he smiled, the skin nearby crinkled. They were strikingly different from my own narrow green eyes. I supposed Isaac couldn't have been much more than twenty-five or so, but he had definitely spent a fair share of time in the sun, as he had a very harsh tan line where the sleeve of his shirt fell. He produced a business card and a pen from his back pocket and jotted a phone number on the back before handing it to me. I took it cautiously, glancing at it before stuffing it into my own pocket. "Well, Lucia, I'm glad to be your first acquaintance this time around. That's my personal cell, so shoot me a text or call me if you need any help with this big job of yours."

I nodded politely in agreement, as Isaac started for the tractor. "I just might have to take you up on that."

Isaac turned back as he walked, moving backward for a few moments. "Oh, and I'll be back to fix that rut soon!" I chuckled quietly as he raised a hand to me, climbing into the cab and taking off toward the field behind the house.

I went back inside, cringing at the sound of the door squealing open. I started a mental shopping list, oil at the very top. I pulled Isaac's card out of my pocket and turned it over. It was a card for a sales associate named Jessica Harvey with Agricore Industries. Isaac had scrawled his number on the back in messy blue ink. I opened my cell phone, adding his number to my contact list under *'Isaac Y. - Neighbor?'*.

I closed the phone and stuck it back in my pocket, scanning the entryway and kitchen. Both rooms were almost as disgusting and ravaged as the rest of the house, but seemed like the most sensible places to start the cleanup. I walked through the large, wood-trimmed entryway and into the kitchen. The linoleum on the floor had once been a cream color, but had turned yellow with age despite so many years sitting untouched. The light-wooden cabinets were open, but appeared mostly intact, yet the countertops had yellowed similarly to the floor. I approached the sink, turning the handle on the faucet. Pipes groaned, and the spout made a coughing noise before spitting out a short spurt of brown water with black flecks and other shrapnel. The stream picked up and became clear but lasted only a few seconds before slowing to trickle and stopping altogether. I turned off the faucet, hopeful that the lack of water could be contributed to the well needing electricity to function.

To my left, the refrigerator sat silently. I opened the door hesitantly and gagged at the contents inside. There hadn't been much left behind, thankfully, but what was there had long since spoiled and turned black. A single gallon of what was once milk sat alone on the top shelf, the translucent plastic coated with black and green sludge, an inch of the same at the bottom of the jug. Fuzzy green mold rimmed the lid, and the entire fridge emitted a rancid odor. I closed the door, still heaving and clamping a hand over my mouth, starting a mental shopping list. *Oil, gloves, mask.*

I composed myself and moved on to a small wooden door at the back of the room, behind which was the closet where we had stored all our cleaning supplies and anything else we couldn't find a place for in the house. The room was hardly big enough to even be called a closet, but it served its purpose. A single light bulb hung from the ceiling, and I pulled the chain. Nothing. *Right. Electricity.* I ran back upstairs to grab my phone to look up the number for the power company. I dialed the number and picked up my flashlight from the floor next to my bed, heading back downstairs as the call connected. I discussed pricing and setup of the electricity with a ditsy woman as I dug around in the closet for usable cleaning supplies. After a few painfully slow minutes, I had successfully set up the power and scraped together a box of large garbage bags, a broom, dustpan, bucket, and an old sponge mop. With a day or two to wait for the electricity to actually kick in, I was determined to make the most of the daylight.

###

As dusk fell and the light inside the house faded away, I decided on a grocery run to kill some time and pick up some fresh cleaning products and food. I walked Sasha quickly before letting the pup back into the house. Then I grabbed my car keys and headed into the front yard to my car, which, I was quickly reminded, was still secured tightly to the back of the U-Haul truck.

I stared at the dolly under the front of my car, examining every connection point before setting about unhooking the chains underneath the vehicle. Once I had unwrapped them, I moved on to the straps that cradled the front tires. I managed to release one strap from the ratchet and pulled out the loading ramps before moving on to the last strap. I pressed down on the lever, but it didn't budge. It remained steadfast as I leaned all of my body weight down onto it. My hands had become sweaty, and slipped off of the metal lever, sending me crashing to the ground. My left wrist caught the corner of the lever on the way down, sending a bolt of pain up along my scar and beyond, into my elbow. I groaned, muttering various quiet expletives, as I landed on my knees in the dirt. Gravel crunched behind me as I got to my feet, and I turned to see a red pickup exiting the cornfield. The truck approached, angling toward me and bathing the front yard in the bright glow of headlights.

"You okay?" Isaac hopped out of the truck and jogged over to me. He looked exhausted, with dirt covering his hands and parts of his face, which itself was shiny with sweat. As he got close, I could smell dirt and oil on his clothing. I didn't dislike the smell, but hadn't encountered it in years. Dad had been a mechanic and would often come home smelling strongly of motor oil, and during the spring, I would sit outside and watch as farmers plowed the fields around the house, the aroma of fresh earth traveling to me on the breeze. Combined, the smell was oddly comforting.

My face reddened with embarrassment, wondering exactly how much of my blunder Isaac had seen. "Yeah, I'm good, just trying to get this car down. I've got everything unhooked except this last tire strap, but the lever is jammed."

Isaac inspected the lever and tried himself to press it down a few times with no luck. He took a step back and put his hands on his hips in thought before lifting a foot in the air and stomping down onto the lever repeatedly. On the fourth hit, the lever gave way and released the strap, knocking Isaac off balance. He staggered backward several steps before catching himself and looking at me, grinning widely. "Got it!"

I shook my head, unable to keep from smiling. "Thanks, Isaac."

"No problem!" Suddenly his grin dropped. "You're bleeding." He pointed to my hand, which sported a bright trickle of blood that dripped from my middle fingertip into the dirt.

"Shit," I pulled up my sleeve, which had already developed dark stains on the spring-green fabric. The lever had split my scar open cleanly at the corner, the pink edges of the roughly half-inch slit glistening in the light as blood continued to seep from inside. I pulled the sleeve back down and pressed down on it with my other hand. When I looked back at Isaac, he was staring at me questioningly. My face reddened once again. "I don't have anything here. That's actually why I was unhooking the car in the first place. Grocery run."

Isaac mouthed an 'ah' and turned for his truck. "I might have something that'd get ya to town and back, at least. Let me look." I followed and watched as Isaac dug around under the passenger seat. After a few moments, he pulled out a small blue first aid kit. He held it up and turned back to me, chuckling. "Dad always said to keep one in the truck. I've just never gotten to use it." He popped the red clip open on the handle of the box. "C'mere."

I did as I was asked and extended my arm, which Isaac reached for. He rolled my sleeve back up and studied the damage. "Old scar, huh? They can be a pain in the ass sometimes." He removed an antiseptic wipe and gauze pad from the kit before grasping my arm to clean it. His hands were rough, filthy, and strong, but also surprisingly warm and gentle.

I could feel my face once again becoming hot, and I looked down at the gravel as Isaac cleaned and covered the cut. "Yeah, it's from a car accident when I was a kid. The hand has lost some sensation, but it's not too bad most of the time."

Isaac didn't say anything right away. He wrapped and taped the gauze, carefully unrolling my sleeve and handing me a wet wipe from the glove box. "There. All better." He smiled and I couldn't help but mirror it as I cleaned the now-dried blood from my hands.

"Thank you." I checked the time on my phone and cursed myself for getting such a late start. "I'd better get going before Pat's closes."

Isaac nodded and closed the door of his truck before starting around to the driver's side. "Yeah, you'd better. Helen likes to hop off the register before closing time actually comes." He laughed and climbed behind the wheel, waiting with the headlights shining toward my car until I had gotten in and pulled the car off the dolly. Then, Isaac backed up and continued down the driveway to the road with me close behind. We went separate ways. I was headed to Whitehill and Isaac headed toward Coalwick.

Pat's Country Mart was a small, quaint grocery store nestled between Duran Family Pharmacy and Cari's Coop Confectionary in historical Main Street, Whitehill. The red-brick storefront was almost a perfect square compared to the buildings surrounding it, which both extended much further into the sky and housed apartments above the businesses inside. A badly faded, frayed, green and white striped awning stretched over the sidewalk, below an equally distressed wooden sign that read 'Pat's' in giant red lettering.

The aisles inside were packed tightly and seemed much narrower since the last time I had visited the store. I combed through the merchandise, unable to find any oil, so I made a mental note to start a list for a later Walmart run. For the time being, I settled on items to sustain Sasha and me for the next day or so until the power kicked back on. I settled on peanut butter, bread, a tin of cashews, a case of bottled water, plastic silverware and plates, and a bag of apples for groceries. I also picked up a small bag of dog food for Sasha and a new mop, rags, bleach, disinfectant spray, and a duster. I could find a pair of rubber dish gloves, but not a mask. I'd made it halfway to the checkout before remembering the gauze still wrapped around my arm. I turned back and picked through the limited first-aid options that Pat's offered. After grabbing a box of large Band-aids and a bottle of peroxide, I hauled my purchases to the front, where a frail-looking elderly woman, Helen, sat on a stool behind the checkout counter. Helen had worked at Pat's since long before I had been born, and she was always a friendly face when my mother and I stopped by to shop. I placed my items on the belt before turning back to Helen, who was staring at me intently. I stepped to the other end of the counter near the register.

Helen smiled. "Do you remember me?" She began scanning items as I reached into my back pocket for my wallet.

I nodded, "I do. You were here when my family used to live outside of town."

Helen continued scanning, still grinning. "Yes! And you went to school with my grandson, James!" She punched a few numbers into the register before giving me the total. "You were just a little girl the last time I saw you. I could never forget those eyes of yours, though!".

I handed Helen my debit card and thought back to every James I could remember going to grade school with. There were only a couple, but I couldn't place which one might have been related to Helen. I nodded in confirmation, anyway.

Helen helped me put everything into bags and walked out to the car with me to load the trunk. "I'll have to tell my James that you're back in town! I'm sure he'll be happy to hear it. He had such a little crush on you back then. It's so good to see you again, Lucy."

I didn't correct her. I thanked Helen and closed the trunk, dropping into the driver's seat as she made her way back to the front of the store. Helen waved as I backed into the street and pulled away.

6

I sat on my knees on the floor, scrubbing at a patch of thick, brown gunk in the corner of the kitchen. It had taken nearly two full days, but I had finally deep-cleaned the entryway and nearly finished the kitchen. The power had been restored the day before and had made the process much easier, as it allowed for progress to be made later into the night. It also fixed the water problem. I had finally gotten the refrigerator clean after copious amounts of dry heaving and one full vomit. It was empty, aside from the bottled water as I hadn't been back to the store since Pat's. I had also pulled every dish from the cabinets and piled them in and around the sink, adding dish soap to my new shopping list. I had found an old bottle, but over the course of thirteen years it had evaporated down to a blue soapy goo at the bottom of the bottle. I sat back on my heels, frustrated as I glared at the filthy patch of linoleum. For all of my scraping and scrubbing, it had barely changed. Sweat beaded on the back of my neck and on my forehead, and I wiped it away with the back of my arm.

A knock at the door provided a welcome distraction. I stood and went to the door, unlocking the knob and cracking it open a few inches. Isaac waited on the porch with a small paper bag. "Hey, Isaac."

Isaac was still dirty from the field, and he grinned as I opened the door fully. "Hi," He extended the bag to me. "I wanted to stop by and bring this to you. My mom would roll in her grave if I let a new neighbor go without a . . . " he looked down at his clothes, covered in dust and oil, " . . . mostly proper welcome."

I smiled. My mother had often had similar notions when it came to new neighbors, even though when our 'neighbors' moved in they were almost always at least a mile away. My mind drifted back to many a house call, with baskets of muffins or Pyrex dishes of casserole. I turned the bag over, letting the object inside roll out into my hand. It was a small, white mason jar with a green ribbon tied into a bow around the base of the lid. The round, green label read *Prairie Hills Farm-Raised Honey*.

Isaac shifted his weight from one leg to the other. "It's local. The farm's actually only about four miles from h–", Isaac was cut off as he began to cough. He doubled over as the coughing became more and more violent. After a moment, the fit subsided, but his voice remained raspy. "Sorry. The dust tends to get to me once in a while."

I stepped to the side of the door. "Come in and get some water." Stepping into the kitchen, I grabbed two bottles of water as Isaac came inside and shut the door behind him. "I'd offer you the choice of tap water, but the well water out here is disgusting." I handed him a bottle, and he took a large gulp as we sat down at the small, foldable dining table in the back corner of the entryway.

I took a sip of my water as Isaac fidgeted, picking at the dirt underneath his fingernails. "So you lived here before, huh?" He looked around, taking in the disastrous state of the living room.

Even though I had had no part in making the mess, embarrassment prodded at me as my cheeks blushed. "Yeah. It wasn't destroyed like this when we left, though. Right after my mom died, my dad basically just dragged my sister and I out of here one day. We went to Tennessee and just didn't come back. Everything was left behind." I chewed at my lip, waiting for Isaac to say something.

"Hm. What do you think happened? With the leaving, the mess, and all." He continued scanning the area.

"I'm not really sure. I was nine when we left, still casted up. My parents didn't get along all that well, as I've come to learn. I sometimes wonder if my dad was just itching to leave her and the house behind, so my mom dying gave him the perfect excuse. He could have come back without me knowing. I stopped living with him when I was seventeen and haven't spoken to him since." Dad's face popped into my head; how upset he had seemed the day I left. At the time, I had felt that leaving was the best option for everyone, but since the news of Dad's death, I had been questioning myself.

Isaac's face scrunched up a bit. "Casted?" He nodded to my arm, which was now covered with a fresh Band-aid. "Was that the accident you mentioned the other night?"

I grabbed my wrist, my stomach tightening. "Yeah. I was with my mom. She was taking me out to Colorado for my birthday. We'd just made it out there and," I swallowed a lump that was rising in my throat and covered my face with my hand. "You know," my voice cracked, and my eyes burned as I fought hard to keep myself from crying.

Isaac was quiet, either taken aback or giving me space to collect myself. I calmed, pinching the bridge of my nose. I dropped my hand and raised my head to look back at Isaac, who was looking back at me with saddened eyes.

I looked back down, ashamed of my compulsive need to over-share. "I'm sorry. That was a lot to dump on you." I stared at the table for a while, fiddling with my hands, before once again raising my face. I half-expected Isaac to be gone; on his way out the door. But he was there.

"It's okay, really. You don't have to suffer in silence." Isaac stood after a long and awkward moment, slapping his hands lightly on the table as he rose. "Well. How 'bout we see if we can make that tap water any better?"

I jolted awake in a cold sweat, another dream shaking me to my core. "Fucking nightmares," I hissed, swinging my feet over the side of the bed and flipping open my phone to check the time. Four-thirty-two in the morning. Sasha woke too, and I picked her up as I stood and walked over to the window. Sasha nuzzled up against my neck as I gazed out at the front yard. A light snow had begun during the night and had dusted everything in a glittering white powder. A single large white tube light hung from a power pole in the middle of the yard, adorned with thick, black wires that extended from the pole to the side of the house, just below my bedroom window. They hung lazily, the slack swinging back and forth in the breeze. I watched, wondering where those wires went to power the whole house.

Movement caught my eye as a dark sedan crawled down the road. I attributed the lack of speed to the new snow but felt uneasy because of the early hour and the state of the vehicle itself. Shadows danced across the paint, outlining a myriad of dings and dents. The distant glow of the yard light did little to dispel the camouflage of the darkness across the road, and I couldn't quite make out the exact color of the car. However, I noticed that the hood had been replaced with a much lighter colored one. The car continued on its way before slowing to a stop at the corner of the property. I blinked hard to refocus my vision and leaned closer to the window. "What the hell are you doing, dude?" I mumbled, "There's no intersection there."

Before I could finish the statement, the driver accelerated hard and sped off. I could hear the engine revving from inside the house and brushed off the uneasy feeling that had crept up on me. My forehead felt tight, and I forced myself to relax the muscles that I hadn't even realized I'd been tightening. Sasha snuggled in tight as I laid back down on the bed with her, drifting back to sleep.

I lay on my stomach on the living room floor, using an arm to sweep under the couch and bring the debris out so I could sort through it. I shoveled load after load of receipts, photos, change, and old toys into the open until the space underneath the couch was clear. One last look revealed a missed item, and I reached back under to grab it, pulling it out.

I trembled, my heart racing as I gaped down at the beige claw-clip in my hand. Many nightmares replayed in my head as my breath became shaky and uneven. I could once again feel the blood pouring over my hand from the clip, see it soaking into the carpet beneath me. I willed my fingers to open, but they remained frozen around the plastic, which dug into my skin as I squeezed ever harder. My grip tightened, and I watched in horror as the bandage fell off my wrist and the scar ripped open fully, my hand contorting out of place and my tendons peeking out of the gash.

The clip snapped, the sound releasing me from my stupor. I dropped the pieces to the floor and snatched up my wrist, which was still bandaged and intact. The carpet was clean, save for the items I had cleared from under the couch. My eyes darted around the room, which was quiet. I scooped everything from the floor into a trash bag without sorting it, and grabbed Sasha, desperate for fresh air. I clipped on her leash and stepped onto the porch with her, still working to slow my breath. We walked into the yard, Sasha hopping through the once again green grass, which had grown taller than she was. I shuffled through, following the path that I had walked before, where the grass had been tamped down a bit. Sasha hadn't figured that trick out yet and stuck to forging her own path through her personal forest. We crossed the driveway, and I inhaled deeply, the cold air soothing my panic a bit.

I snuck a glance at the field behind the house. Isaac stood next to a massive, green combine with a younger man. My glance had not gone unnoticed, as Isaac turned and raised a hand high above his head in a wave. The man next to him stared at me, as though trying to place me in his mind as someone he recognized. He waved as well, less enthusiastically than Isaac had. I waved back, my heart skipping a beat as I glanced at Isaac. I looked down, cracking a smile and walking back to the porch. I stomped off the small layer of snow that had collected on my shoes, shivering as a crisp breeze blew in from the field across the road. My sweatshirts would be no match for the Iowa cold as winter approached.

After letting Sasha into the house, I checked my pocket for my shopping list, finding it crumpled up exactly where I left it. I locked the door and walked to my car, rubbing my hands together for warmth. I pulled out of the driveway and turned left, mindlessly flicking at the radio buttons as I started the twenty-minute drive to Stratset, where the nearest Walmart drew traffic from most of the county.

As I pulled into the parking lot, people ambled across the main lane in small, staggered groups, making it impossible for me to drive through at a reasonable pace. I signaled, hoping to turn into a lane of parking spaces and get out of the crowd. I found a place and parked further away from the door than most cars. I crossed my arms, stuffing my hands into my sweatshirt sleeves as I walked.

An inviting wave of warm air enveloped me as I walked through the door. I pulled a cart from the receptacle and began my shopping, removing the list from my pocket, opening it up, and pressing it flat against my hip to smooth it out. I hit the clothing section first to look for a coat, scores of sweaters and jackets reminding me that this would most likely be the most time-consuming part of my trip. After searching through rack after rack, I found a plain, black puffer coat that wasn't too extravagant. I tossed it into my cart and moved on to groceries and, most importantly, oil. I made quick work of the rest of the list, ready to get out of the store, which was busy for the middle of a weekday afternoon. Deciding I had gotten everything I needed and had had enough of the public for the day, I made a beeline for the front of the store.

I checked out with a tall teenager who appeared she was about as ready to go home as I was and steered my cart at a speed-walk back out into the cold, all the way to my car. I dropped my bags two by two into the trunk and swung the cart into the corral right next to me. My breath was visible in the frigid air as I slammed my car door shut behind me, settling into the freezing seat. I buckled my seatbelt and started the car, checking the rearview mirror as I reached up to switch into reverse. As I looked into the mirror, I noticed a familiar vehicle parked directly behind me, two rows back and running. An exhaust cloud billowed behind the black sedan, which was well beaten, fully tinted and sporting a white hood. My heart lurched as I pulled out in a hurry, tearing toward the back exit of the parking lot. The other vehicle followed at a more leisurely pace. I pulled onto the street and hit the first stop light as it turned red. I glanced into my mirror to find the sedan still behind me, with one car between us. When the light turned green, I took a left turn, skidding as I straightened out onto the next road. The other car continued to follow, tailing me all the way out of Stratset and fifteen minutes toward Coalwick. On the outskirts of Coalwick, it turned off, changing direction. My heart continued pounding as I drove, waiting for the car to return to my tail but it never did. I pulled into my driveway, breathing manually to slow myself down. I laughed nervously, disappointed in my delusion. "Other people live here too, Lucia." Still, nerves rattled me as I carried my groceries inside.

7

Aluminum rattled under my feet as I hauled box after box to the edge of the U-Haul, creating a row of boxes i could reach before hopping out of the truck and beginning the grueling task of toting them inside. One by one I transported sixteen boxes of junk into the entryway of the house, dropping the last onto the table and flopping my upper body over the top of it in exhaustion. My face came to rest on the top of the box, my cheek squishing with the pressure and pushing my lips out into an exaggerated pout. The cardboard was cool on my hot skin, which had become red and sticky with sweat, warmed by better weather and exertion. My hair was not much better, I realized, reaching up to lift the thick, sloppy braid off of my neck. I rolled my eyes upward, raising my eyebrows to see ahead of me without picking up my head. I glared at the staircase, irritated by the realization that many of the boxes now needed to go to the second floor, where the bedrooms could serve as storage for a long while. I let out an exasperated groan and shoved myself up from the table, trudging through the front door and back to the truck. I climbed up onto the back edge of the cargo area and reached up to grab hold of the strap that hung from the sliding door, stepping backward and carefully down to the ground with the door in tow. As I wrenched the latch closed to seal in the furniture I couldn't carry, gravel behind me crunched in the driveway as someone turned in.

I turned halfway around and raised a hand as Isaac's red Dodge RAM rolled in, blasting heavy-metal and hauling a small, black enclosed trailer. I turned the rest of the way around when, instead of continuing on to the field, Isaac came to a stop partway down the drive next to the rut he had dug. I pursed my lips, raising an eyebrow as I watched him. He stepped out of the truck, bouncing his head and playing air drums as he sang quietly. He didn't seem to even notice me while he continued to jam out to his music, stepping onto the back tire of his truck like a stool to pull a shovel from the bed of the vehicle.

I continued watching with a playful smirk, bursting into laughter when Isaac turned around and nearly jumped out of his skin. "Jesus!" He doubled over, holding a hand to his chest and roaring with laughter. When he caught his breath, he stood back up, face beet-red.

I couldn't contain my grin. I had almost thought I'd forgotten how to smile so widely, and it felt both strange and wonderful to have rediscovered the skill. "Death metal, huh?"

Isaac shrugged. "Yep. Why? Not what you were expecting?" He winked and stepped toward the rut, re-distributing the dirt and gravel with the back of the shovel until it looked almost perfectly flat.

The smirk stayed on my face as I crossed my arms and leaned against the side of the U-Haul. "I don't think I know what I was expecting. But no, I guess not metal."

Isaac grinned, tossing the shovel back into the truck bed and moving to the back of the trailer. "I guess I'm full of surprises." He opened the trailer, unlatching the lock at the top of the tailgate and guiding it down into the gravel to create a ramp. I walked over to him as he entered the trailer, which was full of lawn equipment. Isaac climbed onto the seat of a bright-green riding mower and fired it up. The blaring rumble grew louder as he backed the mower down the ramp and into the driveway.

"What is all this?" I shouted, straining my voice to compete with the racket of the mower. "I can't ask you to take on this disaster."

Isaac tilted his head, switching off the engine. "Good thing you didn't, then. I made an executive decision after watching you and your pup trying to get around out here." He got off the tractor and went back into the trailer, hauling out a weed whacker as well. "You didn't make this mess," he motioned to the yard, "and you shouldn't have to break your ankle in a hole you can't see or fill your skin with stickers either."

I threw a hand to my hip and shifted my weight defiantly. "At least let me help you."

Isaac's eyes crinkled as he broke into another grin, putting up a hand and shaking his head. "Nope. No. I didn't bring enough equipment for two of us, anyway." He stuck his tongue out at me and waved me away. "Go keep up what you were already working on. I've got this. I'll let you know when it's done."

I sighed and looked at him, defeated but grateful. "Thank you, Isaac. Really." Isaac nodded, still smiling as I turned for the house, stopping on the porch. "Take breaks once in a while and come in for some water, okay? Door's unlocked." Isaac threw up a salute and picked up the weed wacker as I stepped inside the house.

I paused in the doorway, chewing my lip. I turned into the living room and peeked out the window. Isaac had set to work knocking the grass down to a more manageable level that he could mow over. He still had that infectious smile on his face, even as he worked. I felt my face go red and put my hands over my cheeks, turning from the window. I couldn't help smiling as I shook my head and rolled my eyes, moving back to my stack of boxes in the entryway. I studied them for a moment before deciding they would stay put for now. I decided instead to work on my parents' old bedroom. I collected an armful of cleaning supplies including wipes, a duster, and garbage bags, padding through the living room to a sliding door behind the stairs. The door sat half open, as it had when we left years before. I opened it the rest of the way and stepped inside.

Built-in cabinetry lined the wall to my left, interrupted in the middle by a low vanity. The mirror was still plastered with photos of Carlie and I as children, and one photo of my parents together on their wedding day. To the right, my parents' king-sized bed sat unmade and untouched for more than a decade. The pillows still caved in at the center where their heads had rested the last time they slept there, and the blue duvet crumpled pitifully at the end of the mattress. Much like the upstairs and living room, the room looked as though a tornado had been through the closet and cabinets. My heart sank slowly as I set my items on the bed and opened a garbage bag. I started with the closet, laying out all of the clothing on the bed and removing shoe boxes full of old school supplies and photographs from the shelf above the rack.

I bagged up my dad's clothes and set them up against the wall before taking a seat on the bed next to my mom's tower of tops. I picked up the first shirt, a pale-yellow blouse with a V-neck collar and cap sleeves. Mom used to wear it often, usually to work on Mondays. Yellow was her favorite color, and she liked to wear it on 'gloomy' days to be a bright spot for her students. She was well loved in the classroom, by students and coworkers alike. The next top was another familiar one; a blue Whitehill Blue Sharks t-shirt that was several sizes too big for her. She had no ties to the Blue Sharks, Whitehill's summer tee ball team. The shirt had come from a thrift store in North Carolina. Mom had been so surprised and excited to find something from our area so far away that she had snatched the shirt from the rack with no regard for the sizing or price. Tiny holes dotted the front where the buttons of Mom's jeans had pinched the shirt up against the kitchen counter time and time again. I brought the fabric to my face and inhaled. It was faint, but I could still smell her vanilla perfume around the collar. After folding it, I set the shirt aside to keep for nighttime and continued sorting the rest. In the end, I kept four of her tops for myself and marked the rest for donation.

After about two hours, I had removed and sorted nearly everything. Only one box remained in the top corner of the closet. I took a step into the shallow closet to reach for it, and as I did, the floor beneath my foot shifted. I stepped back, and it shifted again with a quiet *thunk,* as though the floorboards below the carpet had come loose.

I dropped to my knees and felt along the floor, back into the closet, where I found a gap between the wall and the edge of the carpet at the corner. I put a finger into the gap and the carpet pulled away easily, not tacked down like the rest of the carpet was along the edge of the wall. I pulled the carpet up as far as it would go, revealing a large, square cutout in the floor with a board loosely fit over it. I removed the board to find a safe hidden beneath. I sat back on my heels, puzzled. The safe was electric, with a keypad but also a space for a key in case of battery failure. I stood and walked through the entryway and kitchen to a pantry that Mom had converted into a combination laundry-office space. An L-shaped desk sat flush with the corner of the room, the other corner occupied by a washer and dryer underneath a long, white shelf. I pulled the chair from the desk and sat down, reaching underneath and feeling for the key to open the single drawer in the center. Mom had always kept keys and important documents in the desk, so I hoped to find either a code or the key for the safe. Instead, I found a large manila envelope stuffed to the brim with papers amidst stacks of sticky notes, miscellaneous screwdrivers, and what I surmised to be every pen in the house. Letters, I learned as I dumped the contents of the envelope onto the desk.

The letters dropped onto the desk in a flurry. I shuffled them around, briefly examining each one. Almost none of the letters appeared to have ever been folded into a smaller envelope. Every letter was dated in the top left corner, and I again flipped through the pile to arrange the sheets in order by date. The oldest dated back to March 1997, had been sent once or twice per month, and each contained a body of only a singular date and time followed by either 'drop' or 'grab', and signed simply 'D'. This pattern continued up until October 22nd, 1999. The letter on that date was a bit different; a threat addressed directly to my mother.

10/22/99

Sarah,

I don't put up with thieves. You have one month.

I'm with Skinner: "The consequences of an act affect the probability of its occurring again."

Don't learn this lesson the hard way.

D.

I set the letter aside and continued reading through. The frequency of the letters became simply a morbid countdown, increasing to once weekly until they reached their climax at a daily warning for the last week. The last letter came on November 28th, 1999. As always, the letter was both dated and signed, this one also addressed to my mother as the first threat had been. My blood turned frigid in my veins as I read and reread the message printed in a large, angry, frenzied scrawl.

11/28/99

Sarah,

TIME'S UP.

D.

I stared at the page, continuing to read the short note over and over again as my brain short-circuited, trying to make sense of what could have possibly provoked such an obsessive show of rage. D, whoever they were, had branded Mom a thief and wanted her to 'learn a lesson'. But for what? My heart raced, pounding loudly against my ribs.

Carlie's face popped into my mind suddenly, her words burned into my brain. "She had him stressed out beyond his limit. All the time! You never understood because you were so young, and she spent SO much time doting on you." Had she known about the letters, or what had inspired them? Had Dad?

"Lucia? What's goin' on? You okay?" Isaac's voice broke the silence, which had become incredibly dense around me.

My eyes darted to the doorway, where Isaac stood sweaty and red-faced with a worried expression. I blinked hard and took a breath in a pitiful attempt to compose myself, realizing that tears had escaped my eyes and were falling down my cheeks. "Yeah. Totally." I turned the chair slightly toward him, wiping the water from my face and putting on a fake smile. "What's up?"

Isaac raised an eyebrow as he looked at me, obviously suspicious. "Look," he began, "I don't know you all that well, but your face is a terrible liar." He approached me and laid a heavy hand on the back of my chair.

I looked up at him, suddenly feeling guilty for icing him out. Before I fully realized what I was doing, I had switched into over-share mode once again. I handed him the stack of letters, my hand shaking as I spilled my guts, filling him in on everything: Mom's death, our trips during my childhood, my moving out of my Dad's house in Tennessee, everything that came to mind as I thought back to my decade-long spiral. And now the safe that had led me to find the letters.

Isaac sat cross-legged on the floor next to me, inspecting the letters and listening intently as I rambled. When I had finished, he looked back up at me and moved to set the letters back on the desk. "Do you think that safe has something to do with these?" He flicked his wrist, snapping the papers as he spoke, before placing them on top of the rest of the stack.

I shrugged, relieved that he didn't find my tangent to be totally crazy. "I don't know. I found it under the carpet in my parents' closet while I was cleaning it out. I actually came in here looking for a code or key, or something. I found these instead." I laid a hand on the letters as I spoke, monitoring Isaac's expression.

Isaac furrowed his brows in thought, his eyes darting side to side. "What do you s'pose we could bust it open? If you're okay with that, of course."

I thought for a moment before letting out a single puff of air, almost jealous that I hadn't come up with the idea first. I raised my eyebrows. "That could work. Do you have the tools you'd need to do it?"

Isaac nodded. "I should. I'll take a look tonight and bring what I can tomorrow. Can you show me the safe?"

I led Isaac to the bedroom and pulled the carpet back, once again revealing the secret compartment beneath the floor. He studied the safe door, poking and prodding at the hinges and latch, likely deciding what tools it would take to break into the steel door. I sat back and watched, completely ignorant when it came to anything mechanical. Eventually, Isaac covered the floor again and stood, reaching a hand out to help me off the ground. I accepted it, my heart fluttering as I did so. *Cool it, Lucia,* I scolded myself.

I saw Isaac out, stepping onto the porch after him. My eyes widened and jaw dropped at the sight of the lawn. The ragged, overgrown grass had been replaced by very short, smooth turf. Isaac had had a point. The yard was dotted with the occasional dip and hole, none of which I had noticed. I rolled my ankles one after the other as I imagined what it might feel like to step into one of the craters by surprise. I turned to Isaac who examined the lawn as well, his face plastered with a smug grin. He glanced at me, trying to read my expression without my catching him. I did, however, and his smile widened further as he dropped his face to the ground in embarrassment.

"Isaac this is insane! How did you do this so quickly?" My mouth remained agape as my gaze bounced from him to the yard and back again.

He shrugged, still beaming. "Raw talent." He tilted his head quickly, "I also love mowing. That helps too."

I chuckled in disbelief, remembering just how terrible the place had looked just a handful of hours before. "You have got to let me pay you." I reached into my pocket, looking down as my ring snagged on a hole in my jeans.

Isaac's smile dropped. "Yeah, that's not happening. Absolutely not," His voice got more distant as the statement went on, and I looked up to see him jogging to his truck, giggling like a child. "Bye, Lucia! See ya tomorrow!" He waved as he climbed into the driver's seat and started the engine.

I huffed, freeing my hand and crossing my arms. "Unbelievable." I wiggled my jaw back and forth, unable to disguise my smile as Isaac backed out of the driveway and honked as he pulled onto the road.

8

Total darkness enveloped me, frigid air stale in my lungs. I felt trapped in a seatless black box theater. A mist of heavily muted yellow light layered the expansive space, allowing me to see a bit further into the blank, black abyss surrounding me. It was deadly quiet, and a sickening sense of discomfort surged from my feet, rapidly crawling towards my stomach and chest. My scalp prickled as I frantically studied my surroundings, or lack thereof, praying for anything to break up the nothingness. I soon got an answer to my prayer as a soft grinding sound became audible in the distance. I turned slowly toward the sound, scanning the horizon. Nothing. The sound continued, warping to seem as though it was behind me once again.

I turned back to find a misshapen body sliding slowly along the ground. It was my mother; a horrible, disfigured version of her. Her head hung limply, dragging the ground as she crept along. Her auburn hair, once silky and well-kept, was a bloody, gory mat plastered to the side of her head, which itself had caved in almost completely. Bright crimson oozed from the socket where one eye should be. The other eye remained fixed ahead, glazed over with a milky-white film, completely devoid of life. Each limb jutted out at a different grisly, unnatural angle. Shiny, slimy bits of bone peeked out from behind torn flesh, quivering with each movement as she pulled herself along the ground with one arm that was in slightly better shape than the rest of her. A massive, ornate wooden door materialized ahead of Mom's crawling corpse, which kept a steady pace despite its battered and putrid state. The door rumbled open as she inched ever closer, fingernails splintering off and bones fracturing further with nauseating muffled, wet popping noises. I watched, frozen in horror as she disappeared through the door, which slammed shut behind her with enough force to rattle the ground beneath me.

Suddenly my hair stood on edge, my skin tingling with the feeling of a presence behind me. I turned around to face the source of the unsettling sensation. My stomach clenched as a bright flash of light blinded me. As quickly as it had appeared, the light was gone, and the environment around me had changed; no longer a never-ending pit of darkness. I was standing in the sanctuary of a church, an unexplainable wave of comfort washing over my body. A long aisle stretched out ahead of me, cushioned by spongy, maroon carpeting, and flanked on either side by rows upon rows of chestnut pews. The air was warm and fresh, filling my lungs and allowing me to breathe deeply. Simple, golden chandeliers hung from lengthy chains on the high, arched vault ceiling. Low light cast the room in a beautiful amber glow. I closed my eyes, reveling in the reprieve. My break was short lived, however, as the presence behind me returned, a bone chilling wind joining it and raising goosebumps on my arms.

Terror crept back into my body as presence propelled me forward, as if the wall behind me were closing in. I protested, digging my heels into the floor in vain. Still, I slowly approached the stage, which was adorned with a myriad of flowers surrounding a mahogany casket that I hadn't noticed. The lid was open, revealing a much more complete version of my mother. She looked gorgeous, peaceful, dressed in a vibrant, canary yellow dress. The square neckline framed her collarbones perfectly, and she would have loved the playful, puffy sleeves that rested lightly on her shoulders. Mom's hands rested one on top of the other on her stomach, her nails trimmed cleanly and painted a soft beige-pink. Her favorite ring, her daisies, rested on her finger and shone in the light. I reached a hand out to touch hers, but was horrified to be stopped by Mom's icy hand latching onto my wrist like a vice.

I gasped, my eyes shooting back to her face, which was now staring back at me blankly. "Wake up," she whispered. She sat up, her body remaining rigid and her eyes boring through me. I opened my mouth silently, unable to force out any sound. In a matter of seconds, Mom's skin began to turn gray and peel away, revealing muscle and bone beneath. With a stomach-turning crunch, her skull caved in, forcing her eye from its socket. It slid down her cheek and hung limply from the nerves before snapping off and rolling the rest of the way to her lap, leaving a trail of blood in its path. "Wake up," she repeated, her voice becoming hoarse as she began repeating the phrase in quick succession, "Wake up. Wake up. Wake up. Wake up."

Another voice, which I recognized to be my own, joined in from behind me. Hot breath filled my ear as it screamed, "WAKE UP!"

I woke up with a start, my right hand reaching for the ring on my left. I looked down, Mom's silver daisies still safe on my finger. I ran my fingers over the ring, wishing it still sparkled the way it had when it was new. Sasha snored at my feet, unbothered, as I removed them from under the covers and got out of bed. I stretched my back out, bending down to touch the floor with my palms. I stood back up and walked to the window, leaning forward and pressing my forehead against the cool glass. I scanned the yard absentmindedly until an abnormality caught my eye. Poking out from under the roof of the porch, the black sedan sat idling, a cloud of exhaust billowing out next to it. Darkness and the porch almost entirely hid it, but the white hood reflected the beam of the yard light, giving it away. My mouth went dry, and I felt as though I could throw up as I stared at the car, frozen with panic. I stood there, my breath coming in ragged gasps as I waited for the car to leave, but it didn't. The distinct squeal of the front door cut through the silence, and the pit in my stomach grew impossibly deeper. My brain clouded by fear, I dove for the floor under my bed, stopping and reaching up to my bedside table for my phone before sliding my body into the tight space. I just barely fit but was grateful for the bed skirt to help hide me.

I flipped my phone open with shaking hands as heavy footsteps traversed the downstairs of the house, items crashing and clanking around as someone rummaged through them. I dialed 911 and listened to the line ring. A dispatcher had just answered when the footsteps stopped at the bottom of the stairs, soon drawing closer as they climbed toward me. I whispered a desperately quiet "Please help," before ending the call and squeezing my eyes shut hard, trying to think. I opened them, switching to my messages and scrolling down to select Isaac's name and typing frantically.

<u>You</u>: Theres rmeone in m house. Help.

I closed the phone carefully, praying he would read the message despite the late hour, or that my call to the police could be traced from the few seconds I stayed on. The footsteps outside had reached the top of the stairs and made their way all the way down the hall, now entering the room with me. I could hear Sasha whimpering above me and I held my breath as the uninvited guest made their way throughout the room, rooting around in the closet and dresser.

I could see the outline of their feet as they approached the bed, clicking their tongue and beckoning to Sasha as she continued to cry. A rough man's voice spoke to her, "Hey there, where's your momma?" I swallowed hard, my heart threatening to beat a hole in my chest. *Ding!* My phone alerted to a new text, and the room went silent for a moment, soon broken by a chuckle. "There she is." The shadows on the other side of the bed skirt grew as he knelt down to lift it. "Thirteen years." He shot a hand under the bed, grabbing onto my shorts and pulling. I gripped the leg of the bed as he dragged me halfway out before the material tore, giving way and causing the shorts to slide down to my knees. He readjusted his hand placement, this time sinking his fingers into one of my thighs before letting go of the bed skirt and taking hold of the other one as well. I shrieked as he pulled me the rest of the way out into the open and dropped to his knees, straddling me. "I've been looking for you for thirteen years."

I thrashed around under his weight and screamed as he eyed me up and down, his dull blue eyes full of a nauseating mix of hunger and satisfaction. "Who the fuck *are* you?" I howled.

He leaned down, placing a hand on either side of my head. A large hunting knife protruded from one fist, and my heart skipped a beat at the sight of the blade. I fell quiet, looking back to the man's face, which was framed by wiry, salt-and-pepper hair and was contorted into a look of feigned offense. "I'm hurt that your mom never mentioned me. You two were so close. And we worked together for so long." He continued studying my body, stopping on my wrist and grinning, revealing a mouth full of discolored and rotting teeth. "But you have my marks all over you." He reached a hand down, fingers dragging across the skin of my thigh, landing on the scar there. The man traced the scar slowly upward to my groin, and I flinched, recoiling from his touch. Worst-case scenarios flashed through my mind until he removed his hand, placing it my wrist, still smiling.

"What do you want? I swear, you can have it. Please just go!" I continued to fight against him, adrenaline coursing through my veins, my heart pounding out of my chest.

The man's eyes darkened as he answered, "I want my money." He raised his knife from the floor, pressing the cold steel against my cheek. Electricity crackled across my skin where the blade rested, and I stopped resisting.

"What money?" I panted, my mind racing as I tried desperately to have a clear thought. Despite the severity of the situation I was in, I found my brain completely empty, all recent memories a muddy blur. A clarifying bolt of pain traveled up my arm, and I screamed in agony, looking to my left wrist. It was still clamped down under the man's large hand, but he had moved to press his thumbnail into the freshly healing split, tearing it wide open once again. Blood pooled in the wound, spilling over the sides around his thumb, where a faded tattoo lined the webbing of his hand. I couldn't read it fully, but I could make out a 'J'. The rest of the ink had bled, leaving it illegible in the low light. My eyes watered, widening as an idea struck me. "There's a safe," I choked, dragging in a gulp of air, "downstairs in the bedroom."

The man's filthy teeth made another appearance as he flashed a sinister smile. "Let's go take a look." He yanked me to sitting by my wrist before taking a fistful of my hair and pulling me to standing. Sasha barked and howled as he hauled me from the room and down the stairs. I cooperated, eager to give him what he needed to leave and get him out of my house. He pulled me into my parents' bedroom without direction from me and shoved me to the floor in a heap at the end of the bed. I landed with a grunt as my ribs scraped down the edge of the bed frame, groaning as an immobilizing pain blossomed over my side. I moved a hand protectively toward the tender flesh but the man redirected me as he grabbed onto my arms, crossing them and pinning them to my chest with one hand as he reached into his pocket. He produced a large zip tie and tied my hands together, pulling it so tightly that it cut into my skin. I cried out as the sharp plastic dug into my still-bleeding wrist. When he was satisfied with the knot, he looked back at my face. "Where?"

"In the closet. Under the carpet." I watched as he half-crawled to the closet, tearing at the carpet until he revealed the hideaway underneath. He laughed, tossing aside the wooden cover. "I knew it was still here. I even thought about asking that pretty, blonde sister of yours, too. Where is she, anyway? Once I'm done here, I still have some business with her."

"I don't know. I haven't seen her in years," I glanced back to the doorway and stifled a relieved gasp as Isaac crept through, placing a finger to his lips as he stepped past the bed to approach the intruder from behind. He had clearly come straight from his bed, as he wore a pair of green and white flannel pajama pants half-tucked into his work boots with a dark hoodie.

Isaac inched up behind the man, who remained kneeling on the floor as he worked to pry the safe from its hole. Isaac took a deep breath and grabbed the man by the throat, putting him into a tight headlock. The man attempted to stand, instead falling backward and landing on top of Isaac, who groaned with effort as he held on for dear life.

They struggled, rolling around the floor as Isaac strangled the other man, maintaining control. The intruder reached for his knife in his belt, unable to find it in his panic. I continued to watch in horror as the man threw an elbow, the blow landing on Isaac's side and causing him to lose his hold. They each scrambled to their feet, the man retrieving his knife from his belt and swinging it wildly. He missed, and Isaac stood back, his hands in front of himself defensively. Isaac's chest heaved and his eyes darted to me, then back to the man across from him, who stood poised to lunge again.

They continued their standoff for several moments, disturbed only by a booming voice at the front door announcing the arrival of the police. The intruder eyed the window above the bed and made a break for it, climbing over me and unlocking the window before wrenching it open and slicing the screen in one smooth movement. I shouted to announce our location as Isaac dropped to his knees next to me, screaming for someone to chase the man outside, and working to untie my hands. He freed me and pulled me into him without a word, holding my head to his chest and resting his chin on top of it. I winced as my bruised ribs shifted but noticed my own heart rate slowing and breathing beginning to steady as I listened to his through the fabric of his sweatshirt.

As the police entered the room in a cluster, Isaac reached up to drag a sheet from the bed and covered my bare legs with it. He held it up around me as I stood and tried to pull up my tattered shorts with little luck. I held onto the waistband with one hand while Isaac wrapped the sheet all the way around me and held it tight as he ushered me outside to a waiting ambulance alongside two officers. The scene was eerily familiar, red and blue lights blinding me as we walked across the yard. I sat down on a gurney just outside the ambulance doors, my eyes trained on the front of the house as a paramedic directed Isaac away from me to a gurney of his own. The car was gone, fresh tracks in the grass where it had been. "Where the fuck is the car?" I shouted in a panic. "There's two of them! The car is gone, where the fuck?".

A short, older woman with ashy blonde hair pulled into a tight bun approached me with a gentle smile, seeming to ignore my outburst. She wore a navy T-shirt with a star-of-life symbol on the left breast and too-long black cargo pants held on by a black belt. A walkie-talkie on her hip crackled as she reached out to touch my wrist. I shrunk away instinctively before catching myself and allowing her to continue. "Sorry," I extended my arm for her to examine, and she did so gingerly, wiping at the blood with a moistened gauze pad.

"Nothing to be sorry for, dear. You've had quite the night. I'm Liz. We're gonna take good care of you, okay?" She continued cleaning my arm, and I nodded, holding my breath as prickles of fire danced across the newly reopened split. I did my best to focus my attention elsewhere, settling in on Isaac arguing with another paramedic behind us, insisting that he was 'fine' and didn't need to be looked at. I caught on too late to the fact that Liz was speaking to me again.

"What was that?" I blinked at her, my mind fuzzy.

"You're going to need to go into the emergency room. This needs stitches." She pressed a fresh pad of gauze over the spot and I sucked in a breath. I looked back to Isaac, who had won his argument and was now looking back at me, nodding in encouragement as he rounded my gurney to stand beside me.

"Okay," I sighed. "I think I might have a busted rib too, so might as well also have that checked out, I guess." I raised the hem of my shirt just high enough on one side to expose the sore area, where a softball-sized, purple bruise had formed. Liz prodded at the area with a gloved hand, and Isaac laid a hand on my shoulder as I squirmed.

Something popped under Liz's hand and I cried out, instinctively reaching up to grab Isaac. He stepped closer, allowing me to lean into him for support as Liz finished inspecting the bruise. "Sorry, sweetheart. I definitely think you've got at least one broken in there. I'll get you some ice for the ride, go ahead and lay down for me." I did as she said, holding onto my side. Isaac readjusted the sheet to cover me up again and Liz returned with a white plastic bag, which she bent in two until it cracked. She then shook it and wrapped it in a towel before placing it against my side, setting my arm over the top of it to keep it in place. She placed the sheet back over me and stretched several black straps across my body, securing me to the gurney. The paramedic who had spoken to Isaac joined her, and together they slid me into the ambulance.

"I'm right behind you. I'll see you in just a little bit," Isaac called, as Liz climbed into the ambulance with me and closed the doors. She sat down next to me and made a few notes on a clipboard, asking question after question about my medical history, allergies, and the like. I dropped my head back onto the gurney and closed my eyes as I answered, waiting for the interrogation to end.

"Stay awake for me, Lucia. Tell me about your boyfriend back there. What's his name?" Liz stood and leaned over me, flipping open a clear-plastic door to retrieve a blood pressure cuff and pulse oximeter.

"Oh. We're not—," I started, but better of it, "his name's Isaac. What else do you want to know?"

Liz unburied my right arm, wrapping the cuff around it and pumping it full of air. "Oh, I don't know. How did you guys meet?" Like Isaac, she smiled a lot. It seemed tiring, but also left me with small twinges of envy. It was also comforting to have someone positive near me after such a horrible evening.

I looked down at the straps across my chest, my heart fluttering. "Actually, I just moved in. Isaac's a neighbor. He came to say hello on my first day here."

Liz nodded. "He sure seems to care for you a lot." She removed the blood pressure cuff and set it on the seat behind her, jotting a number on her clipboard.

In spite of the situation, the corner of my mouth lifted. "Yeah, I guess he might."

It was quiet, aside from a myriad of *beeps* and other ambient noise. The ambulance bounced around as we hit a large bump and Liz laughed, apparently noting the shocked expression on my face. "We're here! The parking lot is terrible."

I surveyed my surroundings as they pulled me out of the ambulance, the chilled air shocking the skin of my face. Isaac's truck skidded to a stop across the lot, and he hopped out, jogging over as Liz wheeled me through double doors beneath a bright red 'Emergency" sign. In the moment, I couldn't dig up the name of the hospital from my memory. He caught up to us and followed as we rounded the corner, passing a desk with several young nurses behind it. Liz rolled me into an open exam room across from the desk and unbuckled my restraints before she and the other paramedic slid me from the gurney to the bed. I groaned as my ribs shuffled around under my skin. They uncovered me and cold air grazed my skin, particularly harsh on my hip, which had been left bare by my torn shorts.

The room was strangely inviting for an emergency department, walls adorned with yellow paint and fruity wallpaper trim reminiscent of a mid-nineties' kitchen. The sliding door to the hallway was made of clear glass, lined with brown, checkered paper curtains that hung from tracks in the ceiling by plastic cords. A small, gray television stared at me from the upper corner.

Two nurses entered and set to work drawing blood and asking me many of the same questions I'd answered with Liz. Cold metal shocked my skin, and I looked down to see one of the nurses beginning to cut away my tank top. I dropped my jaw and turned my attention to Isaac, whose eyes widened as he realized what was happening. He spun around as they finished up and did the same with my shorts, before replacing them with a blue hospital gown. "You're good, Isaac." I announced. He turned back around sheepishly, and I forced a small smile in his direction, hoping to give him a fraction of the comfort he'd already provided me. I'd never be able to repay him for saving my ass the way he had. Isaac smiled back, and the smallest bit of relief washed over my body.

Soon, a man in light-blue scrubs joined the party. Dark glasses hung from his neck by a handmade, colorful cord, and deep creases marred his forehead. He smiled with tired, but friendly brown eyes, and extended a hand to Isaac and then to me. "Hey, guys. Dr. Juarez," he turned to me, "So we've got some pretty nasty rib pain and a laceration, huh?" I nodded, and Dr. Juarez cleared his throat. "Well, we'll get ya taken care of and out of here. I bet you're exhausted."

I had been surprised to not have cried yet, but tears finally beaded in my eyes, and my lips trembled. "Yes, very." I inhaled deeply, sniffling and blinking back the moisture before closing my eyes against the intense lights above me.

###

Several hours, five stitches, and a chest x-ray later, Isaac and I sat side by side in the exam room on the edge of the bed as a thin police officer entered the room. I recognized her as one of the first officers to enter the house earlier in the night. Her long, messy, copper ponytail had stuck out. Pale freckles dotted her fair skin, and her thick, black police jacket rustled as she sat down wearily in a green, plastic chair next to the door. "I'm Officer Edwards with Whitehill Sheriff's Department. Please feel free to call me Abby, though, if you'd prefer." She paused for a moment, and when neither of us spoke, removed a small pad of paper and pen from inside her jacket. Abby looked at me first, with a sympathy in her eyes that bordered on pity. "Can you tell me a little bit about what happened tonight?"

I fiddled with the green paper scrub top that the nurse had given me to wear home. The getup had come with matching pants and bright-yellow gripper socks filled with loose strings that stuck to my toenails and drove me crazy. I didn't answer for several moments, and Isaac rested a hand on my leg and squeezed. "I don't know," I started, not looking up from my shirt, "I'd had a nightmare and when I woke up, I saw his car sitting in the yard. Then I heard the front door open and I just hid." I gasped and looked up at Isaac, my eyes wide. "Oh my God, I left my dog in there!" I brought a hand to my mouth as I imagined Sasha wandering the house, looking for me after watching that man drag me away from her. Or worse.

Isaac moved his hand to my back, rubbing lightly back and forth between my shoulder blades. "We'll get her."

"What if he comes back?" I made eye contact with Abby.

"I can't say he won't. But we'll have a watch posted at the house for a while. I'd suggest staying somewhere else, at least for the next day or two. Do you have somewhere you can go?" Abby clicked her pen repeatedly as she spoke, shifting her feet on the beige tiles beneath them.

I shook my head but stopped when Isaac spoke up. "Yes. She can stay with me as long as necessary. If she's okay with it," he looked at me and stilled his hand on my back.

I met his eyes, and he flashed a small smile. I swallowed hard and nodded. His hand resumed its rhythmic motion, and I moved my gaze back to Abby, who smiled as she went back to her notepad. Abby scribbled a note, "You said you saw a car. What did it look like?" She leaned in, listening intently.

"It's mostly black, with a white hood on the front. It's dented to hell along the sides, but I've never seen it in daylight, so I've never gotten a great look at it."

Abby began writing again, then stopped abruptly. She glanced at the wall, seemingly in thought, before looking at me. "Wait. You sound like you've seen this car more than once." She raised an eyebrow questioningly.

I puffed my cheeks out, blowing air out of my mouth. "Yeah. It passed my house that night that we got snow a few days back. It was moving super slowly, but at the time I figured the roads must've been slick." I dropped my head back to stare at the ceiling, swinging my foot as I continued, "Then I saw it again at Walmart in Stratset," I sighed, the pieces beginning to fit together in my mind. "It followed me almost all the way back to Coalwick before it turned off. I guess I just wrote it off as paranoia."

Abby nodded, having returned to taking notes. Isaac stared at me with his mouth ajar, incredulous. I shrugged my shoulders and opened my mouth, unsure of what to say.

The interview continued, and I further shared details of the night: the location of the safe and letters, how I'd come to be in the house in the first place, what the man had said about working with Mom and looking for money, and the 'J' tattoo on his hand. Abby noted that investigators would remove the letters and the safe from the house and they would send it off to be opened. I didn't know how much time had passed, but by the time Abby cleared Isaac and I to leave with a promise that Sasha would be checked in on, the sun had started to rise.

Isaac ushered me to his truck and helped me climb into the passenger seat as I kept my arm pinned to my side, steadying my sore ribs.

The inside of Isaac's pickup was a bit on the filthy side, and smelled of dirt and motor oil, much like Isaac himself. I inhaled deeply, letting the scent soothe my frayed nerves. It was a quiet ride back to Coalwick, and by the time we reached Isaac's apartment, I had dozed off. I woke again to Isaac gently tapping my shoulder. "Hey, we're here." I blinked away the sleep and looked around. Isaac parked in the corner of a large cement slab situated behind a red brick quadplex on the edge of town. To the right of the building, cornfields stretched as far as I could see, browning, dead stalks jutting from the ground at varying lengths. The building itself looked old, but in good shape. I unbuckled and stepped out of the truck, beating Isaac, who was making a half-jog around the front of the vehicle. I closed the door behind me and followed Isaac down the narrow sidewalk to the unit on the lower right-hand side of the building. He unlocked the door and opened it, gesturing me through first. I stepped inside and waited for Isaac to join me. He smiled shyly and waved a hand toward the small, dark kitchen. "My penthouse."

Isaac flipped a light switch near the door and the room brightened as a series of dim, flat lights buzzed to life on the low ceiling, which itself was composed of white drop-ceiling tiles in a black grate. A few dark, pressboard cabinets lined the corner of the room under green laminate countertops in an 'L' shape, interrupted only by a dingy, yellowing stove and range hood and a small, single-basin sink. A new-looking, white refrigerator sat lonely on the opposite wall. Hairline cracks covered the yellow-cream walls, which made the room itself look even smaller. Isaac led me to the next room, which wasn't much larger, and sported the same yellowish paint on the walls. A large, gray, well-loved couch took up much of the living room. It looked as though it had once been very plush, but had become thinner and more worn over years of use. Despite its deteriorating condition, I felt I could lie on it and sleep for a week. The only other items in the room were a small end table and a dining table, which served as a catch-all for keys, empty beer cans, ball caps, and more, all surrounding a clunky, black Magnavox television.

"The bathroom is just down the hall," Isaac gestured down a short hallway, segmented by four doors, "and the bedroom is just past that. Here, I'll show ya."

Isaac started down the hallway, but I stayed put. "I'm not taking your bed, Isaac. The couch is more than fine."

Isaac stopped and I could see the muscles in his neck tense as he squeezed his jaw and tilted his head back slightly before turning to me with a smirk. We locked eyes in a silent battle. "I'm not gonna convince you otherwise, am I?" His chocolate eyes betrayed his exhaustion, but still he smiled. It was somehow so infectious.

I lifted the corner of my mouth, failing in my attempt to appear stoic. I remained resolute, however. "Nope. Try again next time." I turned, starting back for the living room. Isaac huffed and rolled his eyes, continuing to the bedroom. He returned a few seconds later with a change of clothes, a pillow, and a light blue-green blanket trimmed in a satin-style fabric.

Isaac tossed the pillow and blanket onto the couch before handing me the clothes. "They're kinda big, but they're all I've got. We can drop by the house for some of your own tomorrow if you're up for it."

I unfolded the t-shirt and sweatpants that he had given me and laid them over my lap. "Thank you so much." I pinched the front of my paper scrub top, which crumpled with an audible crunch. "These are terrible."

Isaac smiled. "They don't look great. Get some sleep, please. You really need it. I'm just down the hall if you need me." His eyes swept the ground as he turned slowly and padded back toward his room.

When I couldn't hear him walking around anymore, I took off the paper pants, sliding them to my knees and kicking them off before replacing them with the Isaac's gray sweats. The pant legs bunched up badly at my ankles, and I tightened the drawstring as far as it would go to secure them around my waist. I crumpled the old pants into a ball and dropped them to the floor next to the couch, moving on to my shirt. I grabbed the bottom of the shirt and peeled it toward my head. As soon as I raised my arms, a painful jolt radiated from my ribs up the length of my side to my shoulder. I cried out, failing to stifle my reaction. The sharp pain turned into a deep ache and I groaned quietly, pinning my arm back down.

Isaac stirred down the hall. "You okay?"

"I might need a little help. I can't raise my arm high enough to change my shirt." Embarrassment rose in my chest as Isaac's footsteps approached, and he joined me in the living room again. "I'm sorry."

"For what? I got you." He went to the table, shuffling through the pile of random items before returning to me and brandishing a pair of scissors. "Sorry to do this to you a second time already."

I turned so he could get to my back. "That'll work, though. I don't plan to keep this shirt." A shiver went down my spine as Isaac began cutting the shirt, the metal of the scissors grazing the skin of my lower back.

Isaac folded the sides of the shirt forward and I grabbed one edge with my good arm, sliding it carefully down over the other to the floor. The air around me felt cool on my newly exposed skin, and I crossed my free arm across my chest in a poor attempt to hide myself while Isaac opened the t-shirt. He rolled it, stretching the sleeve open and sliding it onto my arm as he did his best to look away out of respect. The rest of the process was easy in comparison. Once I was dressed, Isaac grabbed the paper scrubs from the floor and took them into the kitchen, tossing them like a basketball all the way across the room to the trash. "Damn, missed it." He picked them up again and placed them in the can before heading back for the bedroom, pausing and turning to me as he went. "You all set?"

"Yes, thank you. I'm sorry you had to do that." I smiled nervously.

Isaac put a hand on his hip. "Lucia, stop apologizing. I don't mind, really." He flashed me a grin and disappeared down the hall.

I laid down and spread the blanket over my legs. It was soft, despite looking like itchy wool, and like many other things in the apartment, it seemed to have been around for quite a while. I wondered what memories it might hold, if any. How many forts had it topped off? How many laps had it covered during late night movie dates? How many tears had it wiped away? Thin beams of bright light shone through the blinds of the front window, making it difficult to fall back to sleep. My mind continued to race as I turned over, my face hanging over the side of the couch. I stared at the carpet; its short, tan pile interrupted by rivers of bare stitching. It reminded me of the cracks that formed in the dirt during a long drought, like those I had seen in textbooks during grade school. Eventually, a soft snore erupted from the hallway, growing louder over the course of a few minutes. I smiled and buried my face in the pillow, finally lulled to sleep by the rhythmic grumbling.

9

The warm, inviting aroma of fresh coffee roused me from my slumber. I stirred, quickly reminded of the previous night's events by a new sharp pain in my side. I sucked in a breath, groaning as the sharpness faded to a deep, throbbing ache that spread from my hip all the way into my armpit. Rolling over carefully, I could feel my face contort as I forced myself up to sitting. Isaac rounded the corner from the kitchen as I did so, a comically large mug clasped in his hand. "You good?" He handed me the cup, and I held it between both hands, letting the heat spread down my fingers. Isaac stared down at me, waiting for an answer.

"Yeah. I think I'm just sorer this morning since I didn't move all night. It'll get better later on." I brought the mug to my lips, glancing up to meet Isaac's gaze as I took a sip.

He looked less than convinced. "Uh huh." He hesitated, then shuffled back to the kitchen when I said nothing else. The coffee went down nicely, a welcome beginning to the day that I inhaled as I listened to Isaac rifle through cabinets and mumble quiet obscenities all the while. Eventually, he found what he'd been searching for., a triumphant "ha!" punctuating the shuffling of dishes and other random items.

A smile tugged at the corner of my lips as the sink squeaked to life. As quickly as it had turned on, the water stopped. Isaac returned with a white pill bottle and a small glass. I squinted at him. "What did you find?"

Isaac tossed the bottle into my lap and set the glass on the table next to him. "Relief. You should rest today, and these will help you do that."

I picked up the pills, turning the container in my hand. *Norco.* I looked back to Isaac questioningly. "Are you sure? Don't you need them?"

Isaac chuckled. "Nah." He lowered himself gingerly onto the couch next to me. "I've gotten my use out of them. I took them for about two days after I had my appendix out last year." He lifted his shirt to reveal a two-inch diagonal scar just above the waistband of his jeans. "Thankfully, I've become something of a hoarder in my old age and they're still here."

I snorted. "You're in for a long haul if you're already thinking you're old." I twisted the cap from the bottle and looked inside. "How many do I take?"

"I'd start with one and see how you feel. They're pretty strong, so you'll want to stay away from driving while you're using them, but I really think they'll help." He ran his palms down the length of his thighs to his knees and back to his hips tensely.

"Alright. I guess I could go for some relief." My normal reservations be damned, I tilted the bottle, cupping my hand beneath the opening as small, ovular, white pills rolled into my palm. I pinched one under my thumb and dumped the rest back, replacing the top. Isaac stretched over to grab the cup from the table before returning it to me. I popped the pill into my mouth and chased it with a large mouthful of water. The cool liquid contrasted the heat of the coffee I'd last had. The tablet went down easily, and I handed the rest of the water back to Isaac, who returned it to the table. "Thank you. Really." I rolled my shoulders gently. "So, what's on the itinerary for today?"

Isaac eyed me, amused. "Like I said, rest for you. I'm gonna make a grocery run and do a little upkeep around here. Lilah needs her faucet replaced." He gestured to the ceiling as he spoke, and as if on cue, a thump resonated from above followed by an exasperated, poorly-muffled voice. I felt as thought the plaster might rain down as as thunder erupted from above, the sound intertwined with the laughter of what I swore could have been at least four children. As if reading my mind, or my face at the commotion, he grinned and said, "Lots of little feet up there."

I nodded slowly, my heart sinking and bile rising in my throat at the thought of being alone. I swallowed it down, fighting the sudden burning in my eyes. "Yeah, okay."

Isaac stood and rested a hand on the top of my head. "Try to get a little more sleep if you can. I won't be far." He crossed the room, disappearing down the hall. I stared at my feet, my bare toes bruised and adorned with chipping green polish. I guessed I must have smashed them during the other night's encounter. Isaac returned, dressed in a navy flannel and faded jeans that frayed badly at the ankles. He stopped near the front door and balanced delicately on one foot as he slipped the other into a boot before repeating the process on the other side. Groaning quietly, he snatched his keys from a hook on the wall as he swung the door open to flood the living room with sunlight. Isaac shot me a smile and a small wave and stepped outside, returning the room to its previous shadowy state. Slowly, I lifted my legs back up onto the couch, my pain having noticeably lessened. My eyes and arms became heavy as I laid back onto my pillow, allowing myself to drift off to sleep.

When I opened my eyes again, the room had dimmed. The sun filtering through the blinds had softened with the waning of the day. My side throbbed, screaming to me that the meds were no longer in effect. The apartment was quiet, aside from sporadic footsteps above and two muffled voices. I dropped my head to the side, scanning the room and allowing my vision to become unfocused. *What time is it?* It had to be early afternoon. I hadn't been up long when I'd taken the Norco, and I couldn't believe Isaac would have been gone more than a couple of hours. I turned my head, listening to the ceiling above. It was quiet. Suddenly, the knob on the front door rattled and caught before beginning to move again. I watched the knob, which remained firmly locked. My stomach turned as I sat up slowly, careful to keep my noise level low. The movement of the knob stopped and a muffled, inconsistent clicking took its place, as though someone trying to pick the lock. I slid to the floor, stifling a groan as my knees hit the carpet and the impact jostled my body. A severe, deep ache erupted throughout my trunk and right arm. I laid myself flat on the carpet and swallowed hard, lumps having formed in both my throat and gut. My nose pressed into the carpet; I focused on the smell. Old cigarette smoke, dust, and dirt filled my nostrils with little comfort. The clicking continued, and I could feel tears sting my eyes. I buried my face impossibly deeper into the floor, sobbing silently as my lungs burned and my eyes squeezed shut.

CLACK! The door clicked open, the hinges squealing in protest. I couldn't contain the breathy, terrified whimper that escaped me. Just as the hinges quieted and light footsteps replaced the sound, the back door creaked open. I could hear Isaac singing under his breath in the kitchen. Our visitor heard him too. Without wasting a moment, the footsteps retreated more heavily than they'd entered. The door slammed shut, shaking a singular family photo from its place on the wall. It crashed to the floor in unison with Isaac's keys hitting the kitchen table as he noticed the commotion. "What the fuck? Lucia?" His volume grew as he came closer, rounding the corner. He was at my side in an instant, and I flinched as his hand came to rest between my shoulders. "What happened?"

"Somebody was here." I choked. "They picked the lock." I rolled onto my back as Isaac stood, bolting for the door.

"Shit," he growled, swinging the door back open with frightening force.

My heart pounded against my aching ribs and I stared up at the ceiling fan, my breath coming in fragmented gasps as I furiously cursed myself for deciding to come back to town. *You put yourself here, in this shit. By choice, no less! And now you have this man trapped in the middle! Dumbass.* I clamped a hand over my eyes and pressed until I saw stars.

"They're gone," Isaac slipped back through the front door quietly. "Whoever they are." I could hear the lock turn into place and Isaac's heavy footsteps return to the back door. Another lock clicked and he returned. Dropping my hand to my chest, I opened my eyes. They adjusted easily to the low light and found Isaac back by my side. "I'm so sorry."

I looked at him, shocked. "Why?" He'd done so much for me in the short time he'd known me; he'd put himself at risk for a stranger without a second thought. And here he sat, as though this mess was his fault and not mine.

"I shouldn't have left." His umber eyes bored into my own. "I shouldn't have left you alone. I'm sor-"

"Stop" I said with more force than intended, quickly softening my tone. "This wasn't because of you. How would you have even known that he found us?" Isaac broke eye contact, hanging his head. I looked back to the ceiling. "From now on, where you go, I go. Easy fix . . . Right?" I forced a chuckle, hoping to make him feel better as my heart raged against my ribs. To my relief, his tightly clenched jaw relaxed. Isaac nodded silently, his expression still grim and eyes still glued to the floor. "Isaac," I started. He didn't move. "This isn't on you. It's not." Isaac squeezed his eyes shut as I continued, "Please tell me you understand that."

Isaac shook his head, as if trying to push off a bad dream. "Yeah, no, of course. You're right." He raised his gaze from the carpet. "Let's get you up, huh?" He extended a hand, and I accepted it, moaning as I sat up and he supported me with his other arm. I paused, letting my head hang as the room revolved around me. "You good?" Isaac asked quizzically.

I cracked a small smile. "Yeah. Just a little bit dizzy. I should be fine in a second." I had a gut feeling that he wouldn't believe me fully, solidified by the strangled sound my voice had taken on with the pain in my side. It reminded me of a time as a child that I had had the wind knocked from my lungs. In grade school, my favorite place had been the jungle gym, and I was extremely adept at making my way through the bars until I reached the top. A boy from one grade above me had taken to harassing me, especially during recesses. He had found me one day in my usual spot, perched atop the highest rung of the jungle gym with a book in hand. In a matter of moments, he had found his own way up and begun pinching and poking at my sides. I had panicked and fallen, landing flat on my back. Instantaneously, all the air in my body rushed out through my nose. Pain and intense panic had taken its place quickly as I gasped and fought for a breath that, for several minutes, wouldn't come. I remembered watching through tears as the boy had taken off running for his friends, who looked on with shit-eating little grins as they welcomed this jackass back into their fold with high fives and indistinct accolades. When I could finally pull in air again, I filled my lungs hungrily before crawling back under the bars to cry.

My thoughts flickered, this time to the aching in my trunk as I lay in the cold grass feet from my mother's flame-engulfed car. Most days, it seemed all thoughts led to this one. I could vividly recall each sensation: the chill of the dewy grass on my back, the fingers of pain weaving through my chest, the searing heat on my face of the flames that were slowly disintegrating my only friend.

Tears stinging my eyes and threatening to spill, I forced myself up to sitting. Isaac braced me with a hand to my back as I dropped my gaze to the floor. With my teeth clenched, and Isaac's help, I stood. "How did he find me?", I started. Isaac guided me back onto the couch as I continued in disbelief. "Abby is the only one who knows I'm here, right?"

"She's the only one." Isaac sat next to me, face contorted in what seemed like a mix of anger and confusion. "Could he know my truck? Like, from being at the house?" He looked at me and I met his eyes, letting out a deep breath I'd been holding.

"Maybe. He's made at least two trips past the house, so I'm sure he could have come by other times." My heart still pounded in my chest, though I could feel it slowing ever so slightly. "Regardless, we should probably call Abby." By the time the words had left my mouth, Isaac's phone was already at his ear.

###

The sun had long since set by the time Abby left Isaac's apartment that night. She had brought along a deputy who had shyly introduced himself as Ryan Butler before spending the next three hours circling the house, surveying the yard for footprints or other remnants of our visitor. Even with help from Abby, Isaac, and me, the search had come up with nothing. The intruder was long gone, and had left no trace of himself.

Exhausted and sore, I hauled myself to the low stoop in front of the door, nearly falling to the concrete as I sat. Isaac remained in the yard for a few moments, dragging a hand through his hair as he stared at the ground. The porch light cast a buttery glow over him as he finally turned to join me but didn't sit.

Instead, he extended a hand to me "Let's get inside. I think we both could use some rest."

I forced a small smile that he returned. "I don't think I'll sleep too well."

"I don't think I will either."

I took his hand, clamping my other arm down against my ribs, which popped and screamed as he pulled me up with an ease that made my face heat despite the pain. As if registering that rising color that I could feel in my cheeks, Isaac's own smile widened and his eyes flicked to the ground before returning to me. I turned for the door and stepped inside, Isaac close behind.

"If it's okay," I started, "I'd like to take a shower." I stopped short of elaborating, but I had felt disgusting since the encounter in the house, as though rough, dirty hands still gripped my legs and twisted through my hair. As though heavy, hot, rancid breath still lingered on my face and neck.

Isaac nodded, his expression one of gentle understanding. "Yeah. Absolutely." He turned on his heels, aiming for the bedroom, "Let me get you set up."

I stepped into the bathroom, a long, narrow space similar to that of the hallway, not bothering to close the door yet. Yellowing tiles cooled my feet as I shuffled lazily to the vanity, examining my face in the mirror.

I looked awful. Purple ringed my eyes, the normally sharp green of which had dulled significantly. A dark bruise now lines the right side of my jaw from a blow I couldn't recall. A paler hue had overtaken my fair skin, and my ebony hair, once sleek and straight, was now completely disheveled.

A light knock at the doorframe startled me away from my reflection. "Sorry." Isaac appeared, a bundle of clothing and a towel in his arm. His free hand rested in the pocket if his fading jeans, thumb brushing the fabric on the outside. He came to stand next to me, setting the bundle on the counter. "Help yourself to anything in here that you might need." He slid open a drawer near my knee and dug around a bit before producing a small green comb which he laid atop the clothing. "I'll be close by if you need anything."

"Thank you."

He nodded, returning to the hallway and clicking the door shut behind him.

The knobs of the shower squeaked and squealed as I turned them, in search of a temperature hot enough to dissolve the handprints on my skin without burning it. Finally satisfied, I began the grueling process of peeling off my current set of borrowed clothes. The sweatpants feel easily when I loosened the drawstring, but the t-shirt was a much bigger feat. Biting my lip to stifle the sound, a strangled groan broke free as I hoisted one side of the shirt over my head and slid it carefully off my bad side without moving that arm.

The hot water was delightful, easing the edge off of the pain in my muscles as I let it cascade over me. As I washed, the dirty feeling of those hands on my skin began to fade.

I emerged from the bathroom, dressed in a fresh pair of Isaac's sweatpants and a blue button-down flannel shirt that hung loosely down to my thighs. Isaac had changed as well, now wearing a pair of loose black shorts and a black t-shirt. He sat on the floor, leaned against the front of the couch as he flipped mindlessly through channels on the TV. He looked up at me as I took a seat on the couch opposite him, wrapping the blanket there around my shoulders and tucking my feet underneath me. "Feeling better?"

"Very much so," I said, suddenly overwhelmed by my exhaustion and uncurling my legs to lie down while Isaac settled on a football game. Despite the anxiety still heavy in my gut, I managed to fall asleep before I could make out which teams were playing.

I didn't know how long I'd been asleep when I awoke to find Isaac approaching the lamp across the room, TV already turned off. He had flicked the switch on the lamp's power cord and started for the hallway when I spoke, "Isaac?"

He startled and turned back to face me. "Yeah, what's up?"

I paused, the next words caught in my throat. Swallowing hard, I managed, "Will you stay?" I wrung my hands, which trembled ever so slightly, "Out here, I mean . . . With me."

"Absolutely. Just let me grab a blanket." He disappeared down the hall, returning moments later with light gray fleece bed sheet and a pillow with a matching case. He tossed both onto the floor and sat back down, arranging his blanket over his legs before reclining to the pillow. Settling in, Isaac clasped his hands on top of his head and looked up to me. "We'll make it through this, you know." I felt his sincerity, but there was a tinge of worry in his voice.

I nodded, smiling tightly. It was several minutes before I spoke again, "Can I ask you a question?"

"Of course. I'm an open book." He pushed himself up onto one elbow, his face drawing nearer to mine.

"What made you decide to help me?" I asked, uneasy as I gazed at a crack in the ceiling. The long pause that followed made me force a glance down to Isaac.

His brows furrowed in thought. "I guess I didn't really give it a thought . . . It felt right. I'm just glad I made it to you in time." He flashed me a lazy smile, and my chest tightened as I returned it. Part of me still wondered why he'd put his own safety on the line for a near-stranger, though I was certainly grateful for the safety he provided.

With Isaac near, sleep came easier than expected.

10

Days upon days had passed since the break-in. Isaac and I had spent much of the time on the couch, engrossed in football games and reruns of old Hollywood classic movies, and he had spent every night on the floor next to the couch. Next to me. We had just settled into our fourth film of the day when Isaac blurted out. "Wanna do something a little different?"

I narrowed my eyes inquisitively. "What do you have in mind?"

"When I'm bored I like to tinker around here," he started, quickly dropping to an exaggerated whisper, "Don't tell my landlord though." Isaac winked as he stood, extending a hand to me and seeming to read the confusion on my face. "I fix stuff around here when he won't. He hates it." He grinned then, as I took his hand and let him pull me to standing. Isaac led me into the kitchen, stopping at the table to grab a flashlight before dropping to his knees in front of the sink. He flung open the cabinet doors to reveal what even I could identify as plumbing in dire need of help. Not a single pipe in front of us was free of duct tape, and a large bucket had been wedged beneath the lowest point. Isaac handed me the flashlight and reached into the back corner of the large cabinet space, a new pipe in hand that he turned to me and held up. "This has been sitting in there for months, waiting, calling to me." He chuckled and rolled his eyes as he turned back to the mangled tubes, "I swear I can hear it at night sometimes."

I found myself a seat on the floor next to him, switching the flashlight on and shining it into the darkness of the cabinet. "How did you learn to do this stuff? You have to be pretty good at not breaking shit if you still have a lease," I laughed.

"Well, it's a lot of trial and error. My dad started to teach me a few things when I was a kid, but my ability to break shit is a big part of why he stopped." The end of Isaac's sentence was strained, as he fished a large wrench from under the sink and struggled with a large nut connecting two of the pipes. "The rest has been internet videos and luck."

I watched intently, amused. "Do you just keep all your tools under there?"

"Yep. Not a lot of storage here." Isaac turned his head to me, still on his hands and knees amongst the dripping plumbing. "Now pay attention, or you won't learn anything." He grinned and returned to his work.

"I can't see much except for your ass," I laughed, admittedly not unhappy with the sight. "Besides, I doubt I'll ever have a use for the skill set."

Isaac snorted, "It would be useful as a new homeowner. But suit yourself . . . and enjoy the show, I guess." He wiggled his hips and laughed.

My smile flattened a bit as I thought about the house, but I said. "Yeah, I guess it would be. But I'm not even sure I'm gonna stick around long term. After . . . everything." My heart dropped as Isaac's shoulders drooped slightly. "I just don't feel as safe right now. But I haven't really made a decision yet. Not until we hear from Abby."

"That makes sense." The words were cold. Isaac repositioned himself, now laying on his side halfway in the cabinet. "I can't say I'd feel too safe either after what you've been through." He continued working at the nut until it finally came free and he set to twisting the second one at the other end of the pipe. We sat in silence until Isaac finally emerged from under the sink and turned to me, his characteristic warm smile still present. "All done." He stood and stepped to the back door, old pipe in hand. In one fluid movement, he opened the door and tossed it outside. As he closed the door, I could hear the clatter of the pipe hitting other metal. He noted my watching. "I save scrap metal. Puts a couple extra bucks in my pocket here 'n there."

My ribs ached in protest as I moved so stand. Isaac reached down, hooking an arm through mine to hoist me up. "Thanks."

"You got it." He started back for the living room.

"Isaac."

He stopped and turned back toward me as I shuffled toward him. My voice wavered as I spoke. "I like it here . . . with you." I glanced to the floor, picking at the skin around one of my fingernails. "I do. I just don't know what to do if we can't find whoever is after me. Or even after that, if we do."

Isaac tilted his head slightly, studying me. "Do you really think it'd be safer to be on your own? Someplace you don't know, with a stranger trying to track your every move?"

"I don't kn—,"

"Because it's not." His eyes darkened. "All you'll do is run forever. Alone." He didn't break his gaze as he continued, "I don't want that for you."

My eyes burned. "What *do* you want for me?" Anger burned in my chest at the unfamiliar version of Isaac that stood before me.

Isaac sighed loudly, exasperated. He was quiet for a moment, seemingly searching for his next words. He dragged a hand through his hair, his fingers catching on knots as they passed through. "I want you to be with people who care about what happens to you. Where you'll have help if he comes after you again."

"But he knows I'm here. It's just a matter of time before he tries to get in again. Hell, he made it in here once already!" I shuddered, the sound of the door squealing open still burned into my brain. "I hate having to be a sitting duck, waiting around for him to strike while Abby and her team try to track him down. I hate that I've gotten you stuck in the middle of all of this." My hair hung loosely to my waist, and I twirled a piece of the end around my finger, inspecting the frayed and broken strands as I awaited Isaac's response.

He answered quickly. "You didn't 'get me stuck' in anything. I wanted to help you, and I still do. No one deserves this." he gestured toward the front door as his voice and eyes softened a bit. "Especially not to go through it by themself." I couldn't help flinching as he took my hand in his own. "If you want to leave, I won't stop you. But please at least give it a few weeks. Let Abby work the case for a little longer."

I considered, staring at our intertwined fingers before meeting Isaac's gaze. "Fine."

"Fine . . . and we don't have to just sit around and be helpless." He smiled ever so slightly, releasing my hand.

I returned it to my hair, this time running the strands between my fingers. "What can we do?"

Isaac returned to the living room and I followed closely, sitting next to him as he plopped down onto the couch and sunk into the cushions. "We can talk to people in town, I suppose. See if they've heard or seen anything."

"I'm game. Anything to try and move things along." I leaned back, resting my head against the fading slate fabric. "Where do we start?"

Isaac mirrored my position as he thought, before popping his head back up. "I say we start with Helen."

I gaped at him. "Helen?"

"She knows everybody in town, just about."

I shrugged, tilting my head to the side. "Alright. When can we go?"

###

Helen's house was exactly what I'd always pictured a little old lady's being. One story high and painted a soft, birds-egg blue, the tiny house was adorned with ornate, black shutters and matching window-boxes filled to the brim with flowers that had long-since died under the snowfall. Barren shrubbery lined the sidewalk in front of the house, broken only by the low porch and dandelion door. Isaac stepped onto the porch, I on his heels, and rang the doorbell.

As we waited, I craned my neck to see the edge of the roof overhanging the porch where we stood. "Do you think she'll answer?" A white strand of Christmas lights dangled from the roof, the twinkling lights barely visible in the daylight.

Isaac followed my gaze before turning to scan the street behind us. "Oh, she'll answer. She's almost always home if she's not at the store." We had passed Pat's on the way into town, Isaac pointing out the absence of Helen's car in its usual spot by the front door. "It may just take her a minute to get to the door."

Sure enough, almost as soon as he'd said the words the door swung open, the wreath of greenery hanging from it jostling about at the movement. "Isaac!" Helen's soft, squeaky voice rang out as she leaned out of the doorway to wrap her arms around his neck. Her eyes drifted to me and Isaac caught her as she nearly lost her balance. He righted her small, frail body as she paused, then grinned at me. "Hello again, Lucy."

Isaac opened his mouth to say something, and I laid a hand on his back to stop him. "Hi, Helen. How are you?"

"I'm great, dear. Better yet with visitors!" Helen stepped back from Isaac and started toward the door. "Come in, come in! It's freezing out here." She stepped inside, gesturing for us to follow, and we obeyed. A wall of heat collided with me, the heavy air laced with hints of vanilla and cinnamon. I wondered if Isaac felt the same weight as we entered Helen's tiny, dimly lit living room. Helen turned slightly as she shuffled slowly toward the kitchen, a bright, open doorway on the far wall that showcased only a refrigerator littered with photographs and papers under brightly colored magnets. "What can I get you two to drink?"

I was suddenly too aware of the dryness in my throat, of the anxiety tangled in my gut. I glanced to Isaac, who grinned back at Helen with an ease I envied as he replied that water would be fine and turned to me. I nodded, and an awkward beat later added, "Yes, water would be great. Thank you."

Helen smiled warmly and disappeared into the kitchen. As glasses clinked and the faucet turned on, Isaac brushed the back of a hand against mine. I looked over and found him watching me, mild concern lighting his eyes. "You alright?," he mouthed.

I forced a smile, nodding once and flashing him a 'thumbs up' that I dropped quickly, just in time for Helen to round the corner with two glasses of water in hand. Isaac stepped forward to meet her and took the cups before gesturing for me to sit next to him on the fading teal couch along the front wall. He set the glasses down on the coffee table, careful to grab two glass coasters that rivaled the intricacy of the shutters outside as he eased himself onto the couch. I mirrored his movements, watching Helen do the same into a well-worn leather armchair nearer the kitchen doorway.

"So," Helen began, sipping from a beaten-up stainless steel coffee cup, "what brings you two out today?"

By the grace of whatever watched over the universe, Isaac spoke first. "Lucia was attacked." An audible gasp escaped Helen, and I squeezed my eyes shut, opening them only once I'd turned away as Isaac continued. "Someone broke into her house last week and. . .," he paused, "it's important that we find out who did it. They hurt her pretty badly, and it doesn't seem like they're going to stop until they've done worse."

I could feel Helen's stare as she studied me, studied the bumps and bruises on my face that, though fading, I was sure were still visible even despite the low light. She had to have noticed them immediately, must have wondered about them the moment she saw me. Counting the small table lamps that dotted the walls, I trailed my eyes back to Helen, meeting her now misty gaze. "Sweet girl." She pressed a hand to her heart as she looked back to Isaac. "What do you need to know?"

"Anything, really. It would help to know if you've heard anyone talking about Lucia around town, or of anyone that sounds like her." He paused, thinking. "Or maybe even if you've heard of or seen any new, odd, or interesting characters in town?"

Helen nodded in thought, setting her cup aside and sliding her thinly framed glasses up onto the top of her head to rub her eyes. "I've not heard of anyone permanent moving into town, but there's been a bit of an influx of travellers stopping through. I suppose that could be odd, just given that. . ."

". . . Coalwick is so tiny and out of the way?" Isaac cut her off.

"Exactly. Most of 'em are staying down at that campground by the creek behind the Ferguson place." Helen peered out the front window past my head at a little girl riding by on a purple bicycle. "Couldn't say why one of them might want anything with you," she nodded in my direction, "but they'd be the only 'new' folks in town that I know of."

As Isaac chimed back in, my attention shifted to a small framed photograph on the side table next to me. A tiny, bleach-blond boy sat cross-legged in the lap of a young woman with light brown hair. They perched on a dock, fishing rod held together in one of each of their hands, a large fish dangling from a line strung through the other. The boy's mouth stretched from ear to ear in a massive grin. An indiscernible feeling churned in my gut as I took in the photo, as though I'd seen its subjects before. "That's my James. He used to love fishing with his momma when he was a boy."

I glanced at Helen before turning back to the picture. "Do they still fish?"

It was quiet for a moment before Helen spoke again. "He does. Sometimes. Nettie hasn't gone with for years now, though."

"Why'd she stop going?" Silence fell over the room. Even Isaac seemed at a loss for words as I shifted my gaze to him. His own remained fixed on Helen, who fidgeted with her fingernail in her lap. The knot in my stomach tightened until she finally spoke.

"She's gone. One day she was here, the next it was like she fell off the face of the earth." Helen brushed uncomfortably at her skirt with her palms before continuing. "Nettie was a great girl, but she fell into some bad habits, spent a lot of time with some," she paused, as though searching the room for her next words, "less than desirable crowds. Her boyfriend at the time made them all look like saints. But she swore up and down that he loved her. Proved it with bruises and split lips, when he wasn't dragging her into the city to sell her for drugs." Helen's voice cracked, and Isaac sprang to his feet, handing her a box of tissues from the coffee table. "Thank you, dear."

Isaac returned to his seat next to me and continued in Helen's stead. "Jamie was just a kid, and he doesn't talk about it much, but there was a day that Nettie dropped him off here and just," he shrugged, "didn't come back." Isaac looked to Helen, who still dabbed at the corners of her eyes with a tissue, and went on. "The most he'll say is that she would call every so often for a little while, but after a few months she stopped." He scratched at the back of his head before running a hand through his hair. "Who knows if he ever heard from that boyfriend. I'd highly doubt it though."

My heart hurt for the little tow-headed boy. *With* him, at the pain of losing his mother so young. Alive or not, she'd gone from his life. Worse yet, she'd left him by choice. Before I noticed it, a tear rolled down my cheek and I swiped at it with a hand, turning away. Too late. Isaac's heavy hand laid gently on my shoulder, the warmth of it comforting even as embarrassment reddened my face. "I'm sorry."

"Honey, Nettie made her choices. As sad as it is and as much as we miss her, James and I have lived a great life. I hope and pray that wherever she is, if she's still alive, that she is okay. But know that we are okay too." Helen lifted the corner of her mouth in a weak smile as I turned back to face her.

Isaac squeezed my shoulder as though he understood, even if Helen couldn't. I let a hand drift to his knee in a silent *thank you* as he expressed our gratitude to Helen out loud. "It means a lot that you'd take the time to tell us what you know, Helen, thank you."

Helen waved the thanks away with a hand. "No, thank you for coming out to spend some time with an old lady. I just wish I had more to share." She turned to me, shifting to stand. "I'm so sorry you're going through all this." Helen crossed the room, closing the space between us and brushing a bony, arthritic hand across my cheek. "Keep some ice on these bruises, honey. It'll help them fade faster."

11

Isaac crouched on the floor of the entryway, wiggling a brand-new brass doorknob that he'd installed on my door. Nearly two weeks had gone by with no sign of the man who had attacked me. Granted, I hadn't come back to the house more than twice since the break-in, but the car had also been nowhere to be seen. I was almost more disturbed by his sudden disappearance than if he had come after me every day since the first time. I kept watching for his car, waiting for him to find me back, to strike again.

Isaac let his hand fall to rest on his leg. "Hey, could you hand me the deadbolt?" He motioned to a small box on the porch next to my feet.

"Sure." I bent down carefully, scooping up the box. I straightened back up and fished around in my pocket, retrieving my car keys to cut the tape from the top. "Why didn't we get a set again?"

Isaac chuckled. "Because these pieces match just fine and are cheaper together than the set is by itself."

I smiled and pulled out the packaged deadbolt, cringing as the plastic scraped loudly against cardboard. Taking a few quick steps forward, I extended the package to Isaac. He took it and used his pocketknife to cut open the hard plastic cover. I stepped back to my place by the railing of the porch to supervise, but my phone ringing interrupted me. I opened it up, walking into the yard as I answered.

"Hi, Lucia? This is Officer Edwards. Abby, with Whitehill Sherriff's Department. Do you have a second to talk?"

I stopped walking. "Hi, Abby. Yeah, what's up?" I turned back toward the house, where Isaac had looked up from the packaging in his hands. He stood and jogged to me, looking concerned.

Abby spoke again. "I need you to come in as soon as you can. We got the safe open."

I looked at Isaac. "Yeah, okay. We'll be there in an hour."

Isaac raced back to the house to finish putting in the deadbolt.

###

The Whitehill Township Sheriff's Department was situated in the southwest corner of town, inside one of several condemned houses that had each been home to a meth lab at one time. The drug ran rampant throughout the county, beginning in the late eighties, and it hadn't seemed to have met an end in most places. Whitehill, however, was an exception. The election of a new sheriff, Leona Johnston, after Y2K had brought on a wave of drug busts that resulted in the discovery of four low-level manufacturers. The participants had gone to prison, and the houses were condemned. Johnston repurposed one house into a new office and demolished the rest. Run by Abby and three deputies, the department generally covered both Whitehill and Coalwick. I'd long thought this a non-issue with the lack of population across the towns, but given my present situation, I had changed my tune.

We parked in the cement driveway next to two squad cars, which had parked one in front of the other on the right side. Isaac turned off the ignition and stepped out, slipping his keys into the pocket of his jeans as he started for the side door, which was now the main entrance to the large yellow house. I was close behind him, grabbing onto the back of his flannel shirt as I caught up. The inside of the building was much more put-together than the outside, though after more than a decade since its last remodel, the inside was showing its wear as well.

The door stuck as Isaac made his first attempt to open it. Small gaps dotted the perimeter of the frame, showing its poor fit. Where one gap had grown wide, someone had responded with a plywood board; wedging it tightly between the door and its frame. This may have improved the cosmetics of the doorway but made its function much more difficult. Isaac turned the knob a second time and wrenched the door open with a loud groan, as a warm puff of air escaped around us.

We stepped inside and I pinched Isaac in the middle of his back. I saw his smirk forming at the sight of the 'remodel', regardless of when the work had been ordered. The large, open kitchen we stepped into was dark and lacked any built-in lighting. Cheap, poorly fit linoleum lined the floor throughout the room, warping and squeaking as we moved around. He glanced at me and back to the short, unmanned metal desk that sat perpendicular to the door. Isaac shifted impatiently as he looked around the room. I noticed a small, silver bell at the corner of the desk with a sign—Ring for help. I tapped the button on top gently, releasing a clear *DING* which cut through the quiet. Isaac jumped slightly, and I rested my hand between his shoulders. We'd both become terrible at self-regulating and had resorted to making our best attempts to manage each other's nerves. I was bad at it, but Isaac was a natural.

He relaxed a bit as shuffling sounds began in another room. "Coming!" Abby's voice rang out through the room, which had gone silent once again when the bell finished its tolling. Abby popped her head out of the office first, a spray of red hair preceding the rest of her body as she tripped over the high threshold. She lurched forward, catching herself after a few quickened steps that pounded loudly over the floor. "So sorry. Thanks for coming in!" Abby waved a hand toward the room she'd just come from. "Let's talk in private." I looked around at the empty room as we followed.

Abby's office was just as poorly constructed as the rest of the building that we'd seen. The floor remained painfully uneven, and I had to continue holding onto Isaac's shirt to keep from stumbling around as we made our way to two wooden chairs across from her tiny, shoddy desk. The work surface consisted of a flat pressboard box balanced precariously on skinny aluminum legs. It was bare aside from a single file, an old-style gray laptop, and a bronze nameplate reading *A. Edwards*. The air was quiet, and incredibly tense. Isaac spoke first. "So, what did they find?"

Abby jumped back to attention as if she'd zoned out already. "Oh, yes! Sorry, normally our investigator would have these kinds of conversations with victims but he's out of town right now." She flipped open the file. "Terrible time to go, if you want my opinion." She hung her head. "Sorry. Sorry. Let's just get into it." She produced a photograph of the safe, which they had cut from its place in the floor and placed on a white background—a table, maybe. The door was open, and stacks of large-denomination bills lay banded together to the right of the door. An ammunition box and a crinkled paper lay on the other side of the door.

My jaw fell slack, and I reached out to touch the photo, leaning in for a better look. "What is all this?"

Abby slid the photo across the table, and it came to rest between Isaac and me. His face mirrored mine as Abby explained, "Four-hundred-seventy thousand in cash. We're guessing this is the money he was looking for."

I looked at her. "What about the ammo and the paper?" I stuttered, trying to think clearly. "St…start with the paper."

Abby nodded, producing another item from the file; a copy of the actual paper. She handed it across the desk to me. It read:

That thieving bitch is dead. You're next.

Nausea bubbled in my stomach as I read and reread the words scrawled in the same frenzied hand as the letters I'd found in Mom's drawer. Without looking up, I choked out, "Do we know who wrote this? And the others?"

"Well, most of them have prints for the two of you," she gestured to Isaac and I, "Sarah, Sullivan, and a man named Dennis Goodman. That one," she nodded to the letter in my hands, "has only prints for Sullivan and Dennis."

I continued staring at the mostly blank page, my eyes drying out. Isaac picked up with the questioning, as if reading my mind. "Could that be who attacked her? Who is he anyway?" I could feel the floor moving, his leg bouncing rapidly now as the tension in the room rose.

"He certainly could be." Abby retrieved yet another file from the folder. "He's originally from Stratset, but pretty much all we have on him is an arrest record. He was arrested here and there in the eighties and nineties in Stratset; small-time methamphetamine distribution and the like. His latest offense was in Tennessee. He literally just got out like nine weeks ago."

My head popped up and I could feel the color drain from my face as the air in my lungs grew thick. *Goodman.* "What was he arrested for?" My voice shook and cracked as I forced the sentence out.

Abby flipped through the report, sliding a mugshot across the desk to me as she read. He was younger, but very much the same man I'd seen in my house. "Aggravated armed burglary in Orestin back in 2004." She glanced up, then back to her paper. "It was," More flipping. "Residential. One female accomplice shot by the homeowner. I guess they caught Goodman on scene, holding her."

Intense heat rushed up my throat, and I stood, dashing for the door. My chair slid loudly over the linoleum as I went, stumbling across the floor until I reached the exit. I shoved the door open with all my weight, ignoring the cry of my still-healing ribs as I staggered into the driveway and threw up. Someone pulled my hair back as I heaved until there was nothing left in my stomach, nor any oxygen left in my lungs. Tears flooded my face and my heart tripped over itself, beating at an incredible pace. I coughed and choked, swaying off balance before heavy hands gripped my shoulders and directed me to the porch stairs to sit.

I dared a glance to my left, Isaac's legs next to mine on the step. My breath came a bit more slowly as he rubbed circles on my back. "Lucia, tell me how to help." I didn't respond, still dragging in gasps and blinking away new tears. "I'm here. Take your time."

Dad didn't 'just move' us to Tennessee. We were running. *Goodman found us.*

My eyes fluttered as the panic hit a second wind, my chest tightening painfully, my breathing speeding once again. Isaac shifted, his hand leaving my back as I felt the rough skin of his palms encompass my own hands – removing one from its place in my lap and the other from its vice grip on his jeans. I hadn't noticed myself grab onto him. "Sorry," I gasped, my eyes not leaving the ground between my feet.

Isaac adjusted again to keep my hands in one of his own, the other moving to gently raise my chin, bringing my face to his. "Try something with me?" He paused, waiting for me to answer. When I didn't, he tried again, his tone so persistently level and patient. "Hey. Lucia."

I re-focused my vision, which had blurred out to leave me looking through him rather than at him.

"Try something with me." Isaac searched my face, still waiting for an answer. He brushed his thumb across my chin softly, keeping my attention.

"Okay."

Isaac removed his hand from my face, placing it back where it had been between my shoulder blades. "Look around. What are the first five things you can see?"

I obeyed, turning my head to face the cornfield across the road. My field of vision followed the motion a split second behind, as if I were drunk. "Irrigator...Windmills--" I choked, the air catching in my throat as my eyes darted across the bare ground in search of three more answers.

Isaac tapped his fingers on my back rhythmically. "Try looking somewhere else for more. Take your time."

My eyes released their hold on the field and drifted to the driveway of the station. "Cars."

Isaac guided my head back until I looked directly at the sky. The warm sunlight kissed the skin on my face, in welcome contrast to the crisp air. "The sun." A puffy, white face smiled down at me from above. "Clouds."

"Good, good. Okay. Now close your eyes."

I complied. My eyelids had grown heavy. "Okay." My balance wavered and I leaned backward slowly.

Isaac braced me, without losing a beat. "What do you feel? Think about anywhere your body touches the ground, or anything else."

"I can feel your hand over mine." My face scrunched as I worked to pinpoint areas of sensation across my body. "I can feel you tapping on my back."

"I'm glad you've noticed that." I could hear Isacc's smile in his voice. "What else? You got two to go."

"My back hurts. And so does my head."

"Try to relax your muscles in those places." He stopped tapping, pressing his hand flat against me as I manually unclenched my forehead and back muscles. "That's four. Kinda tough, isn't it?" Isaac continued as I nodded weakly, already waiting for the next instructions. "I won't make ya' list any more out loud if you don't want to, but find three things you can hear. Just say 'okay' when you're done."

I listened, hearing nothing identifiable at first. Soon the humming of the outdoor furnace fan stole my attention. Then, a child laughing in the distance, joined quickly by several others. Finally, my own heartbeat in my ears, slowing ever so slightly. "Okay."

"Two things you can smell."

I inhaled deeply through my nose, immediately met with Isaac's familiar cologne of oil and earth. My mind traveled back to the day I'd first noticed the way he smelled. He'd barely known of me eight hours and he'd already stopped to check in on me, and had had to patch up an injury I'd caused on my own. Isaac's hand moving in circles again on my back brought be back to the present, and I recognized a smile tugging at the corners of my mouth. "I don't have a second one."

"That's alright. Last one. What do you taste?"

A grimace overtook my face as the sour, foul aftertaste of vomit came to the forefront of my attention. I raised my head and opened my eyes, squinting at the bright light they'd lost acclimation to.

Abby crouched in front of me, a bottle of water in her outstretched hand. I took it gratefully as she rested her other hand on my knee. "Take a moment and have a drink. We can pick this up another day, maybe we'll have a bit more information by then. Go home and get some rest, please."

I nodded. I was suddenly aware that I had become exhausted. My limbs felt enormous, dragging as if they each weighed fifty pounds. "Thank you." I turned to look at Isaac, repeating myself. "Thank you."

He pulled me in to his side. "Of course. My mom used to use that on me all the time. It's good to practice when you feel yourself starting to spin out. I just wish I could do more."

"Please eat something." Isaac set a plate down between my laptop and me, seated at the tiny two-person table in his kitchen. I nudged it aside without looking to see what was on it, making room for my arms so I could search *Dennis Goodman + Orestin TN + arrest + 2004*. Isaac sighed audibly as I scrolled through the results. The second hit was an article from the Orestin Weekly Reporter.

GOODMAN SENTENCED TO SEVEN YEARS

April 4th, 2005

An Orestin man has been sentenced to seven years in a Tennessee state correctional facility in a burglary case from September of last year. Dennis F. Goodman, 49, was found guilty of aggravated armed burglary in January, and last week was sentenced to 9 years in Frost River Correctional Facility. His accomplice remains at Fairview General Hospital in critical condition. She is not expected to survive at this time.

Homeowner Veta Sanchez, a first-generation American from Chile, states "This is not the justice I expected. I wish he'd spend much longer behind bars. They took the sense of safety away from my home. I can only hope God takes over from here."

Goodman and one accomplice broke into Sanchez's home last year, while she was preparing to go to bed. No motive behind the burglary has been determined, and no items were stolen. Sanchez was home alone at the time, and was able to access her firearm, which she keeps in her home for her safety. Sanchez fired on the intruders, striking Goodman's accomplice in the head. Goodman pulled the unnamed accomplice onto the front lawn, where he was unable to retreat further. Goodman was apprehended at the Sanchez residence at that time, while his accomplice was taken to Fairview General.

--Margaret Yang, Senior Reporting Journalist - Orestin Weekly Reporter

"Huh." I leaned back in my chair.

Isaac looked up from his plate, where he had been picking at a small pile of spaghetti. "What'd ya find?" He stood and came around the table to look over my shoulder.

I pointed to Veta's name in the article. "That burglary that Dennis Goodman went to jail for? He was in my dad's neighbor's house. Veta lived directly to the West of us."

Isaac leaned in to get a better look at the screen, reading. The warmth radiating from him was comforting, especially on such an unnerving day.

I continued. "I bet he meant to hit us but was off." I bookmarked the page, not sure why, and closed the computer.

Isaac returned to his seat across from me. "Why would he follow you all the way back out here instead of staying in Tennessee? Wouldn't it violate his parole to leave the state?" He answered his own question, "I guess he probably doesn't care too much about that, though." Isaac pushed his plate away and sighed, before furrowing his brow. "And how would he even know where to find you after seven years in prison?"

I looked at him, my head spinning. "I have just as many questions, many the same." I pulled my legs up to sit cross-legged in my chair. "I have theories, not facts, though. I'm guessing he's after more than that money by now." I explained Dennis's comment about having business with Carlie after he finished with me. "He probably wants us to suffer. Or die. I just can't wrap my head around my mom being involved with someone like him, though. She was too good." Isaac readjusted in his chair, patiently listening to me talk out my tangled thoughts until I reached his second question. "As far as how he knew to come back here, I have no idea. Luck on his part, maybe? He did grow up here, I guess. The only person who has recognized me, or that I've recognized, for that matter, has been Helen."

Isaac nodded in acknowledgement. "At Pat's, right?"

I grunted in confirmation, picking up my fork and chopping at the noodles on my plate until they became tiny pieces. I couldn't bring myself to take a bite, and every so often I noticed Isaac watching me. Dropping the fork back onto the table with a loud *clink*, I rested my head in my hands.

Sasha rounded the corner happily, having woken from a nap in the living room. Abby had sent an officer to drop her off to us the day after the break in, but she still acted as though she hadn't seen us in weeks every time we came back to the apartment. I stood, patting my thighs. "Wanna go out?"

Isaac followed. He hadn't left me alone for more than a few minutes in quite some time. I didn't mind it. I clipped on Sasha's leash and she led me to the door in a little-dog attempt to take my arm off. Isaac beat me there and opened the door, a piece of paper fluttering in the breeze the motion caused. "If this is another 'inspection', I swe—" He unfolded the paper and stopped abruptly, reaching a hand to the back of his waistband and inspecting the yard. Isaac had carried a small pistol since my coming to stay, just in case. He extended his other hand back to me, signaling me to wait. I took the paper, stepping back and picking up Sasha as I stared at a photo of Isaac and I on my porch that morning. The angle of the photograph and the trees in the foreground made the hair on my arms stand up as I thought about the thick lining of trees on the far side of my driveway.

Suddenly tires squealed in the distance and Isaac snatched the gun from his jeans, holding it steady, pointed to the ground with his finger on the trigger. A large gray, beaten-up pickup whizzed around the corner on two wheels. The driver laid on the horn as they passed, and Isaac visibly relaxed, his tense face turning to one of amusement as he chuckled and put the gun back in his waistband.

"Who the fuck?" I shouted.

Isaac stepped aside and waved me by. "It's just Jaime."

"Jaime?" I questioned as I stepped through the door. "More, please." I scanned the neighborhood carefully, finding nothing out of the ordinary.

Isaac laughed. "Jaime Price. Helen's 'James'. He works with me in the field behind your house. He's sorta our 'mechanical apprentice'. He lives with Helen above the pharmacy over in Whitehill. Doesn't have many friends. Probably because this is the kind of shit he thinks is funny." Isaac puffed air out of his nose and shook his head. Adjusting his jeans on his hip, Isaac re-sized his belt and tightened the clip around his waist. I'd come to learn that Isaac had the type of build that could surprise someone. 'Sleeper build' I think my dad had once called it. In Isaac's case, he was extremely strong from work but hid some of that muscle under a tiny bit of a belly. I smiled as Sasha did her business and Isaac continued. "He's saving up money and experience to go to college in the fall. Wants to be a diesel mechanic, but really, he's more of a lackey for my old man."

I took a few steps toward Sasha, reeling in some of the slack on her leash. "What do you mean?"

Isaac put a hand on either side of the door frame, swaying forward and backward to stretch his shoulders. "Well, we don't have the means to offer him any kind of advancement. Dad keeps him around with vague mentions of a job after college. Stringing the poor kid along, if ya ask me. Pisses me off something terrible."

"That sounds shitty." I slapped the outside of my thigh and whistled for Sasha, watching Isaac's reaction from the corner of my eye.

Isaac nodded. "Mhm. I dunno if Jaime has any idea, or if he's hitched to a dream. He's from a dirt-poor family, and now Helen's all he has left. She sure ain't getting him through college on what she makes at Pat's. Let alone keeping herself alive at the same time."

I took Sasha inside and Isaac followed us, locking the door and dropping the photo onto the table where all things went to die. I unhooked Sasha and she pranced away playfully, ignoring our existence as I sat. "What happened to the rest of his family?"

Isaac plopped down next to me on the couch and fiddled with a bulky, gray remote control. He pressed the power button and the dinosaur of a television stirred to life with a metallic *thunk* and Isaac flipped through channels idly, many of them partially or entirely static. "He doesn't really talk about them. All I've ever gotten out of him was basically the same thing Helen told us; that Nettie dropped him with her some years back and hasn't been around since. I can tell it's a sore spot, so I don't push much. I've known Jaime for two or three years now, and he's never so much as mentioned names. Not even Nettie's. I only know hers because of Helen." Isaac shook his head, appearing disgusted. "Takes a real piece of shit to dump your kid without an idea when, or if, you'll be back. It makes the way my dad treats him so much more irritating."

I swiveled to face him, my knees tucked to my chest, my chin resting atop them as silence replaced his voice. After a beat, I spoke up. "Why don't you say anything about what your dad is doing? To Jaime, I mean."

Isaac dropped his head, his gaze settling on his lap. "My dad and I aren't on the best terms. Best to let him do his thing and stay out of the way." He cleared his throat and went back to flipping through channels, the corners of his eyes reddening.

My stomach sank. My questioning had upset him. I waited a moment, remembering something he'd said to me. "You don't have to suffer in silence, Isaac. I'm here if you want to talk."

Isaac didn't look at me, but I could see him swallow hard and lift the corner of his mouth slightly before nodding. He reached a hand out to me and placed it on my knee, squeezing lightly. "Thank you."

12

"Shit!" I rolled off the couch, snagging my jeans from the floor and racing to the bathroom in one clean motion. "Shit, shit, shit! Sorry, ma'am." I tried in vain to reel in my panic as the woman on the other end of the line waited with the patience of a saint.

Isaac emerged from the bedroom, swiping sleep from his eyes with one hand, clawing through his ruffled hair with the other. His pajama pants sat low on his hips and he reached down with a hand to yank them upward to his belly button, sighing as he tightened the drawstring and listened to my expletive-laden phone conversation.

I returned from the bathroom, holding my phone to my ear with my chin while I tied my hair up in a messy braid down the side of my face to my shoulder, where it ended near the waistband of my jeans. I'd normally wear it in a knot or ponytail, but for me, a braid was easier to maneuver in a rush. "How much do I owe after fees?" I turned to Isaac, who still stood dazed and confused in the bedroom doorway. I pointed to the phone, and he put his hands up quizzically. I motioned for him to get dressed and hurry, and he hopped slightly before turning around to get his clothes. Moments later he returned with a gray hoodie on and his bottom half-dressed, one foot stuck in the pant leg. He hopped down the hall, struggling with the jeans before tripping and falling to the floor. He tried to catch himself on the couch as he approached, but flipped himself over to land on his back on the carpet. Isaac gasped as the wind left him and I stifled a giggle and turned away, despite my frustration with myself. Isaac rested his hands on his stomach and laughed silently, tears filling his eyes as he gasped for breath. After a moment, he shimmied the rest of the way into his pants and stood, still waiting for me to end my call. I did so. "Okay, thank you for letting me know. I'll be in by the end of today."

Isaac watched me as I snapped the phone shut. "What's that about?" He pressed on one of his eyes, still reddened from his laughing fit.

I stashed the phone away in my pocket and crossed my arms. "I'm way late on returning that Uhaul. It's gotta go back today or they'll keep adding fees."

Isaac made a face. "How late is 'way late'?"

I looked away. "Two-ish weeks." When I looked back at Isaac, his jaw was lax. "At this point the fees are just lower than the balance of my savings account. So, we need to take it back before I can't pay for it."

Isaac grabbed his keys from the catch-all table. "Gotcha. Let's get it empty, then."

I let Sasha go outside quickly before letting her off her leash inside the apartment and joining Isaac at the truck. As we pulled out of the parking lot, Isaac opened his phone and punched some buttons, glancing up to the road periodically as he did so.

I looked at him. "Should you be doing that right now?"

Isaac snorted and continued on texting. "Just a quick one. I'm finding out if Jaime can stop by and give us a hand with the heavier stuff today. Then I'm done, I swear." He finished the text and dropped his cell into my lap as I considered his inviting Jaime to help, placing a hand on my side. My ribs had improved quite a lot, but weren't quite finished healing. *Good call, Isaac.* I picked it up, turning it over in my hand. The phone was exactly what I would have expected if I ever had given a thought to what kind of cell phone Isaac carried. The heavy, red, rubber-trimmed Samsung was beat to hell and filthy, dirt and dust crusting into every crack and crevice I could see.

I held the phone up, smirking. "How does this phone even function anymore? It looks like the whole cornfield came home with you."

Isaac chuckled, grabbing the phone back and wiping it uselessly on his shirt. "Yeah, I guess maybe it could use a bath." He shoved the device into his sweatshirt pocket.

We showed up at the house much more quickly than I thought possible, and I hopped out of the truck, eager to get my junk inside and the Uhaul out of my hair. "Come on, lead foot!" I could hear Isaac laughing and as I approached the front door. An officer from Whitehill sat at the corner of the porch and nodded to acknowledge me as I unlocked the door. The officer did the same to Isaac, who let him know Jaime may join us later and to let him by if he did.

My heart sank as I took in the downstairs. Every bit of cleaning, clearing, and organizing that I had done had been reversed. The furniture in the living room was once again overturned and dispersed throughout the room. Vinyl gloves and plastic shoe covers littered the floor amongst the contents of my end table drawers. A single, skinny trail of blood droplets led from the front door through the living room. My wrist tingled, and I reached over to hold it with my other hand as I traced the speckled line all the way to my parents' darkened doorway, where a hazy figure chilled my blood. Dennis' gnarly face protruded from an odd sideways angle behind the door frame, his broken, jagged teeth on full display in a massive grin. His yellowed fingernails gripped the wooden frame tightly, splintering it. Panic flooded my body, freezing me in place, my eyes futilely searching for the lower half of his body.

Isaac's heavy hand landed on my shoulder, and he pulled me to his side. "You know, Jaime and I can handle the inside."

His touch broke me from my stupor and I glanced to his face, then back to the living room. Dennis was gone. "I'm okay. It's just...a *lot*. Especially since I already had so much done," I sputtered, my mind grasping for a reasonable excuse. "Besides, we don't even know if Jaime's coming." Just as I got the words out, a knock on the door startled us both.

Isaac moved to open the door and I shuffled to my place at the front window in the living room. Isaac caught on and called after me. "It's just Jaime, Lucia." He swung the door open wide, gesturing to Jaime to enter. As he came into my view, Isaac grabbed him by the arm and pulled him into a quick embrace, punctuating it with a friendly slap on the back. "Hey, man!"

They separated and Jaime turned to look at me. I recognized him from the field with Isaac, but now that I could see his face up close, he felt even more familiar. This must be Helen's 'James', and he must have gone to my grade school. He seemed younger though, eighteen or nineteen at most, and a shaggy mop of bright-blonde hair topped his head. Jaime's blue, hooded eyes sat slightly deep in his face, giving him a tired look.

Jaime turned to me, smiling. "Hey, Lucia. It's nice to meet you again! My grandma said you were back in town, but to be honest, I had a hard time remembering who you were. It's just been such a long time. You do look familiar, though!" He chuckled shyly, reaching one thin arm across the other to stretch. I imagined that like Isaac, Jaime was likely also sneaky-strong.

"So do you." I chewed on my bottom lip as the room fell silent, unplaceable discomfort settling in my gut.

Isaac clapped Jaime on the back again. "Should we start?"

###

It took the three of us just under two hours to empty the U-Haul and drag everything into the house. I opted to collect the police leftovers and scrub the blood from the floor while Isaac and Jamie covered the bulk of the lifting. Isaac locked the knob and pulled the door shut behind us as we stepped onto the porch. I removed the U-Haul key from my keyring and replaced the rest of my keys in my pocket.

I climbed into the driver's seat and rolled down the window, waving Isaac over. "Hey, can you drive my car, so it doesn't die from sitting?" I pulled my keys back out and handed them out the window. He took them, throwing up a short salute before walking to my car next to the U-Haul.

The drive to Whitehill was slower with me in front. Despite the mileage I had driven in the massive vehicle to move, I had never gotten fully comfortable with its size. Every so often, I'd look up and see Isaac making faces at me in the rearview mirror, probably bored on the longest trip to Whitehill in his life. It was strange to see someone else behind the wheel of my car, but it was oddly difficult to take my eyes off of. *Is that what I look like driving down the road?* I broke from my distraction just in time to make the turn into the U-Haul parking lot. Parking next to the entrance, I shut off the engine and paused, checking every compartment for items I might have left behind. Satisfied, I hopped out and headed inside, wallet ready for the financial nightmare I was about to enter.

An electronic bell sounded as I entered, and a bored-looking teenager sat buried in her cell phone behind a low counter topped with only an old cash register. She didn't move when I approached the desk. "Um. Hi. Excuse me." The girl looked up, annoyed. A bright orange name badge hung crookedly on her white T-shirt. *Brandie.* "Hi, yeah. I have a truck to return." The doorbell sounded again as Isaac entered and joined me.

"Name?" Brandie asked, standing slowly from her chair. She reached under the counter to produce a logbook, which she opened to the most recent page of entries.

"Pierce. Uh, Lucia." I tapped the toe of my shoe on the tile floor nervously, as Brandie inspected the names, keeping her place with a long acrylic fingernail.

Brandie grunted in frustration and looked back up at me. Thick black eyeliner smudged around her waterlines. "When did you check it out?"

"November 29th. But I checked it out in Orestin, Tennessee. I'm actually pretty late getting it back to you guys." I gripped my wallet tightly under the edge of the counter, picking at the trimming around the corners. Isaac grabbed my hands in one of his just as the trim started peeling off. *How does he always know? Am I that obvious?* My breath caught in my throat and my eyes widened, but I did my best to keep my mouth from gaping open as I felt my cheeks becoming hot. *Brandie didn't notice. Instead, she had started for a back room, walking with her shoulders slumped forward at an angle so severe it looked painful.*

Brandie returned a couple moments later, followed closely by a stout woman who looked to be much older than her, and less than friendly. Short, heavily gelled, unnaturally red hair stood on end on the woman's scalp. I checked for a name tag but didn't find one. Conveniently, I didn't need to, as her face was not indicative of her demeanor. The woman extended her hand to shake mine, and I set my wallet on the counter to reciprocate, the fingers on my free hand still entwined with Isaac's. She jerked my hand around wildly, causing my side to ache. Finally, she let go of me. "I'm Stacey. I hear you've got some late fees going on?"

I sighed, "Yeah, unfortunately. Do you take a card?"

Nearly four-hundred dollars later, I had wiped out my bank account, but I wasn't tied up in a rental anymore. Isaac drove us back to the house to spend some more time sorting through my parents' things while we still had daylight. Even with the police presence, I didn't feel comfortable staying at the house past dark while Goodman was loose. Isaac wasn't as worried as I was since he was always with me, but he was respectful of my concern.

We arrived back at the house shortly, parking my car at the edge of the driveway. I tossed my keys onto the table and kicked out of my shoes, padding across the living room to the stairs with Isaac in tow. Isaac overtook me, racing up the stairs two at a time until he reached the hallway, where he stopped and waited for me to catch up. I waved a hand toward the door to Carlie's old room and Isaac grabbed the knob. The door squealed as it swung open to reveal a room packed floor to ceiling with plastic totes. Only the bed and a small pathway to the closet remained unobstructed. Carlie had never let me into her room as a child, and I began to wonder if this was part of the reason for her secrecy.

Stale air and dust stirred up in a rush as we entered, and I shimmied through the stacks to open the single window on the opposite wall. Thick cobwebs and dead bugs littered the windowsill, and I wiped my hands on my pants to no avail, a grimy sensation sticking to my palms. Sunlight poured over the contents of the room, revealing large handprints and finger tracks in the dust on every tote. Someone had rifled through every single one; likely Dennis hunting for money.

Isaac and I each pulled a tote into the hallway, sitting cross-legged on the floor with a box on either side of us. Old greeting cards, yarn, and school crafts had been crammed into the first two boxes, and we came to find that most of the totes were full of much of the same junk that my mother would have saved. Isaac started a stack by the hall window of totes that would go straight to the dump with all of their contents. Very few items made the cut to keep. The light outside was fading as we dragged the last two containers into the hallway. I flicked the light switch halfway down the wall, and dim orange light filled the space as we sat down.

I peeled the lid off my tote to reveal more random items, but Isaac opened his to find it only half-full of yearbooks. "Hey, check this out." He lifted four books from the box and set them in his lap. Each book's cover was decorated with a different maroon and gold pattern; the colors for Stratset Consolidated High School. Several other books remained in the tote. Unlike those Isaac had picked up, these were orange and black; products of Coalwick Grade School. I left them in the box and turned my attention to Isaac's stack, the first of which he had opened to the class pages. He flipped through a couple of pages of smiling teens, almost all dressed in their best picture-day outfits, and stopped. *Juniors - Class of 1978* was printed in ornate lettering at the top of the page, four rows of students laid out in alphabetical order below.

I turned to sit facing him. "Do you know someone from that class?" I studied his face, which I couldn't read.

Isaac continued staring at the page for a moment before he registered my question. "Hm? Oh, yeah." He pointed to an attractive brunette girl in the third row, second from the left — *Denise Scott.* "That's my mom." Her brown eyes were identical to Isaac's and had the same crinkle to the skin when she smiled.

"She's beautiful, Isaac." I laid a hand on his arm and realized how tense he'd been.

He relaxed a little. "She really was. God, I miss her."

My heart pounded as I leaned forward, resting my head on Isaac's shoulder. "Has she been gone a long time?"

"Yeah." Isaac cleared his throat and placed his hand on my back. "She died last month, but she was gone long before that." I pulled back and looked at him. He met my eyes. "Dementia. They diagnosed her about ten years ago. They'd never seen it in someone so young. Not around here anyway. She stopped recognizing us within a few years after that." He closed the yearbook and opened the next; *Stratset Consolidated HC: 1977-78.* He continued as he flipped slowly through the pages. "I thought I was ready for her to go, but then she actually did. It was even worse on my dad."

I put my head back down. "I'm so sorry, Isaac. That must be awful."

Isaac was quiet, moving his hand up to lightly squeeze the back of my neck. He stopped again on the Juniors' page. "Will you show me your mom?"

I smiled, reaching out to turn the pages back to the Freshmen. I scanned the page, looking for my mom's face. "There." I pointed to her photo. Mom smiled widely, her adorable round face glowing with joy as it had always seemed to.

Isaac's face lifted. "I wonder if they knew each other. Your mom kinda reminds me of a family friend that used to come visit before mine got sick."

I smiled, flipping through the pages until I reached the candids, "I have no idea." Grinning high-schoolers covered the pages, in each shot participating in some sort of extra-curricular. I locked in on one photo that featured my mom. Mom stood at the front of a classroom, her arm extended straight above her head to measure the height of a massive model tower. Another girl, equally proud, kneeled on the other side of the tower at the base. She craned her neck to look up at the structure in awe. The girl's face felt familiar, but I couldn't place her. "Do you know who this is?" I nudged Isaac, pointing to the photo as he leaned closer to look.

"I don't think so." He squinted, thinking as he scanned the page for a moment. His eyes shifted and he dropped the book back into his lap, tracing a finger along the caption of the photo as he read, "Sarah Barlowe and classmate Jeanette Price admire their prize-winning popsicle-stick skyscraper, which won first place in height at Mrs. Frost's annual 'Builder Brawl'. April 1977."

"Price," I started "Like Jamie, Price?"

Isaac met my eyes. "Yeah," He paused. "Why?"

I squinted in thought, twisting my back to stretch as Isaac closed the book and placed it back in its bin. "She just looks crazy familiar to me." As I turned, I caught a glimpse through the window and my eyes widened. The sun had disappeared, leaving the sky dark outside the window of the hall. "Shit, we should probably get back. Sasha's gonna freak out."

Isaac set the rest of the yearbooks back in the tote and rolled onto his knees to stand. I took off down the stairs as he called after me, "Hey, wait up. I'm old!"

I rolled my eyes, laughing, but not stopping. I pulled my sneakers on without untying them and grabbed my keys as Isaac grumbled, making his way down the stairs.

When he joined me, I grabbed onto the back of his shirt as we walked to the door. We stepped onto the porch, exchanging goodbyes with the officer there. Isaac took off ahead of me, turning to walk backwards as he approached his truck. "Hey, question. Do you wanna go get some real food tonight? My treat."

I pulled my mouth into a wide grin, glancing at the ground. "Sure. Got a place in mind?"

Isaac waited a beat for me to catch up again. "Well, there are about three choices between Coalwick and Whitehill. We could flip a coin…a couple times."

A chuckle escaped me. "Sure. Let's do that. We gotta check in on Sash first, though."

"Of course." Isaac started in a feigned bravado, "We'll have to change, too. I can't take you to the fine establishments of Podunk, Iowa, dressed like that."

I stopped, placing a hand over my heart, an insincere look of offense etched on my face as I examined my dust-caked outfit. "What? Is there a dress code that excludes shitshow chic?"

13

Honeybee Tavern was packed for a Thursday night by Whitehill standards. Isaac and I had settled on the tiny bar after two coin tosses to rule out the other two options: Harvey's Diner and Third Street Inn, both also in Whitehill. Isaac parked on the street with the other four patrons and hopped out of the truck. He jogged around to my door, which I had just cracked open. Isaac pushed the door closed on me, holding a hand up to the window before bowing and re-opening the door himself. I cringed as he chuckled and slid from my seat.

I lost my footing immediately upon my feet hitting the ground and stumbled, dragging the back of my pant leg across the dirty truck's running board. "Well, the nice clothes didn't last long."

Isaac smiled. "You got further than me." He raised an arm to reveal a large grease stain on the side of his flannel. "Found this right before we left. My church flannel too."

Honeybee faced Pat's Country Mart, just diagonally across the street. The only business in town open past five o'clock, it drew a large crowd; often bringing in three or more cars along with a couple of in-town walking customers.

A small John-Deere lawn mower sat parked on the sidewalk in front of the bar's large picture window, its bright green paint distorted by the yellow and pink neon of the sign Shabove. Andy, Isaac mentioned, was a long-time regular who lived at the edge of town. Andy was old and his physical health had declined, so it was a bit too far for him to walk, but years of excessive indulgence at Honeybee had left him permanently without a driver's license. "No license necessary to operate a mower," Isaac laughed. Part of me conjured a vague memory of the machine sitting in the same spot when I was a child, and I forced a chuckle, though a twinge of pity struck my heart.

Isaac opened the storm-door, behind which a standard residential door stood open despite the chill outside. However, the intense stuffiness inside the building soon explained the unique choice. Seventies country filtered through wall speakers, feeling somewhat disjointed from the name and storefront decor of the business. I had envisioned some sort of pop or electronica, but in Whitehill the country made more sense. The sense of discord was confusing, yet charming.

A massive rustic bar lined an entire wall of the long room, mirrors lining the back of each shelf to create a dizzying double-image effect. The rest of the narrow room was dotted with tables of varying shape and size. Most of the tables were open, with the few people who had gathered at the establishment congregating together either at the bar or at one or two designated tables. Loud laughter erupted intermittently as Isaac and I chose a small two-seater in the back corner.

We squeezed ourselves into the slim booths across from each other. Isaac made a show of wheezing and holding his stomach, which pressed against the edge of the table.

Isaac grinned, proud of his act, and waved as a tall, gray-haired woman approached the table. She wore a black T-shirt with the Honeybee logo and a black server apron that was dusted with flour. "Hey, Isaac! How's it goin'?" The waitress set to laying out two menus and pulled a pair of straws from her pocket, setting them on the table before producing a notepad as well.

"It's definitely goin'!" Isaac smiled politely and looked at me. "This is Polly. I come in here from time to time."

Polly stopped, her mouth agape in embarrassment. "Oh my lord, I'm so sorry! I should've introduced myself! I get so caught up in all the regulars here that I forget we do get new customers, too."

I forced a smile, my leg beginning to bounce on the ball of my foot. I could feel the floor shake with the rhythm and stopped, embarrassed further. "It's okay. My name's Lucia."

Polly grinned, revealing a row of too-perfect teeth. *Dentures, maybe?* "My, what a name! Well, Lucia, can I get you something to drink?"

I made a feeble attempt to scan the menu for the 'Beverages' section, but after a moment searching, I was overwhelmed by the feeling of eyes on me. "Just water. Thanks."

Isaac ordered a beer and Polly shuffled across the floor before disappearing through a set of silver double-doors behind the bar. I looked at Isaac, who was twirling a cardboard coaster around with one finger on the table. "I'm not here that much. Somewhere between you and Andy. Somewhere in there."

I smiled, releasing my jaw a bit and dropping my shoulders. "It's a nice little place." I skimmed the menu absentmindedly. "I'm sorry to be so awkward. I'm not used to going out."

Isaac met my eyes, tugging one corner of his lip upward. "You're doing great." He paused a moment, reading his own menu before spinning it around to show me. He pointed to an item about two-thirds of the way down the page. "I usually get their tacos, but their wings are awesome too…It's all good shit. Get whatever sounds good to you."

"Honestly, tacos sound amazing right now."

Isaac beamed and raised a hand to Polly at the bar. Polly returned, setting our drinks on the table and retrieving her notepad once again. "What are we thinkin'?" Isaac ordered two plates of tacos for us and Polly grinned. "Fantastic choice. Isaac's favorite." She winked at Isaac as she turned to head back to the bar.

Isaac made a face and reached back to scratch at the back of his neck, shaking his head. "That's Polly for ya'. Big flirt, but a really great lady." He was quiet for a moment, taking a large gulp of his beer and watching the people at the bar talk and laugh amongst themselves. Then he looked back at me. "So…have you given any more thought to whether you'll stay in town?"

I stirred my water, watching the ice bob up and down around my straw. Stealing a quick glance back at Isaac, part of me wanted to break down; to tell him that somehow, he had become the only reason I couldn't make a firm decision on the matter. "Not much, to be honest. I definitely don't want to stay in that house anymore." I took a sip, the liquid paving a chilly trail all the way down my throat as my response played over again in my head. It wasn't entirely untrue. Most of my experience since returning to Coalwick, especially inside that house, had left me itching to run for the safety of distance from Dennis. Yet every time the idea of leaving again struck me, the thought of being separated from Isaac sank my heart. In such a short time, he had become a constant part of my life; a comfort that I hadn't yet figured out how to part with.

Isaac nodded, watching me intently. "I can't say I blame you. There's a lot of trauma in there. You have a place with me as long as you need." His lips formed a tight smile as Polly returned with our food. Isaac thanked her and dug in hungrily. I watched him for a moment, familiar warmth rising in my chest.

"The thing is, I don't know what to do with the place. I could probably sell it, but I'm not sure I want to deal with it even that long." I took a small bite, leaning far over the table to catch any pieces that fell. There were quite a few.

Isaac wiped his chin with the back of his hand. "You could burn it down." He shrugged and went back to his food.

I rolled my eyes, smirking. "Right."

Isaac was spot on. The tacos were incredible, but I was tapped out after two of the three that came with the order. I passed my third to Isaac, who was more than happy to finish it.

Isaac wrenched himself out of the booth and I followed. The floorboards creaked as we moved toward the bar. Leaning against the polished wooden countertop, we waited for Polly to join us and ring us up. I put a hand on Isaac's arm. "I'm gonna run to the bathroom quick before we leave." I made another visual sweep of the room. "Where would that be?"

Isaac pointed me toward an alcove at the front of the room. Rather than just an alcove, I found a hallway that extended much further than the space should have allowed. A tiny, single-stall restroom was tucked into the end of the hall, as promised.

When I returned, Isaac had struck up a conversation with one of the men at the bar. As I approached, I recognized Jaime's bright blonde hair.

Isaac grinned when he noticed me and clapped Jaime on the back in a friendly farewell as he backed away from the bar and came to meet me. "Ready?"

I nodded, and Isaac placed a hand on my back, guiding me toward the door. My breath became visible as we stepped outside from the toasty bar. Hugging myself for warmth, I hurried around to my side of the truck, jogging in place as I waited for Isaac to unlock the door. He finally did, and I scrambled into the vehicle. It was little help, though, as the inside of the truck was nearly as cold as the outside. Isaac hopped in and started the engine, turning the heat to full blast as he pulled away from the curb.

We rode in silence for a few minutes before a muffled thumping noise broke the quiet streak. The truck vibrated violently, and Isaac's arms tightened as he fought for control of the vehicle. "Shit. I bet the tire's flat." He slowed, guiding the truck to the side of the road. We had made it over two miles out of Whitehill, the lights of town just orange dots in the distance. Isaac leaned over me to pull a miniature flashlight from the glove box. "Wait here. I'm just gonna look first." He popped the door open, a blast of icy air rolling into the cab as he got out.

I picked at my fingernails as I waited. My stomach churned, and I bounced my knee once again. The reflection of headlights in the mirrors caught my attention, and I turned around in my seat. The vehicle pulled over behind us, the lights blinding me. I could see Isaac stand and raise a hand to the driver and say something, flashing a grin and looking relieved.

After a moment, Jamie came into view, outlined by his headlights. He seemed upset and scowled at Isaac as he approached. Isaac's smile dropped as Jaime spoke. Isaac glanced in my direction, his eyes cold with fear. My stomach sunk and I watched, glued to my seat as they argued, their breath mingling in the air like smoke. I reached into my pocket for my phone, gripping it in my lap with white knuckles.

In an almost imperceptible moment the disagreement became physical, with Jaime landing a blow to the side of Isaac's head, so hard I could hear the impact from where I sat. I flipped open my phone, dialing 911 and leaving it on the seat to call as I opened the glove box, digging for anything I could use as a weapon. Coming up empty-handed, I crept out of the truck and ducked, sweeping my hand underneath the passenger seat until my hands met with cold metal. Thank God. Tire iron in hand and heart racing, I slunk around the bed of the truck.

Isaac had made it back to his feet, despite Jaime continuing to pummel him. "Jaime, stop!" Isaac's words were muddled, his mouth bloody.

I lifted the iron, readying myself to swing, but hesitated as the two men scuffled. I couldn't hit Isaac. Bile crept up my throat, and I swallowed it down as I sucked in a shaky breath. "Jaime!"

Jaime turned, and I lashed out, hauling the iron through the air with as much power as I could muster up. My aim was off, though, and one socket landed on his shoulder, rather than his head. Jaime grunted and stumbled backward before collecting himself and lunging for me as I dropped the iron and steadied my balance from the swing. He collided with me, sending our bodies careening toward the ground in a heap.

My head bounced against the pavement and my vision turned to static as Jaime's powerful hands snaked around my neck. I threw my hands out, clawing for eyes, but finding only air. "Why?" I croaked, tears forming.

My vision cleared in time to see Jaime's face soften. He swallowed hard, his eyes misty. "Please, just let go. This can be so easy." The sour scent of beer wafted into my face as he spoke. I squirmed as Jaime's grip tightened, my airway entirely blocked. My lungs exploded, burning like fire, and my face felt as though it had swelled to twice its size.

I blinked rapidly as the corners of my vision went dark. Suddenly, Jaime let out a terrifying cry and let me go. He collapsed at my side, writhing and whimpering in pain, his hands reaching for a place on his back he couldn't reach. As the air rushed back into my body, I began to regain my faculties.

I sat up, watching Jaime as he continued to struggle, more slowly, as a dark puddle formed beneath him and he began to cry, his eyes developing a distant stare. "Mom. Please." He looked so afraid, like a child lost in an unfamiliar place, his eyes darting around in search of something he wouldn't find. A deep part of me wanted to go closer to him, to comfort him. But I stayed put, frozen in place by the fear that he'd somehow still overtake me again. Minutes felt like hours as his weak whimpers became labored, raspy breaths, then finally stopped altogether.

Isaac stood above me, wavering, a huge, bloody hunting knife in hand. He looked as if a car had run over him. "You need to call your sister. Dennis sent him here. He could be headed back for her." As the last word left his lips, Isaac drew a few ragged breaths, staggered backward, and crumpled to the ground. He landed in a seated position, his back against the back driver's tire of the truck. He waved me on with a hand. "Go. Call."

I scrambled back to the passenger seat, grabbing my phone. My 911 call had ended, and I dialed Carlie's number as I ran back to Isaac. I dropped to my knees in front of him, my cell clamped between my ear and shoulder as the line rang.

I had no idea how much time had passed since my first call to the police, but Isaac pulled his own phone from his belt and opened it. His breathing became increasingly labored, his hands shaking uncontrollably as he tried to dial. Crimson blood streamed from a gash on his wrist as I took the phone from him, icy panic freezing my veins as I took in its black, shattered screen. I took off my sweater, wrapping it tightly around his arm. "Isaac, show me where else you're hurt."

"My stomach." He grimaced as I lifted his heavily bloodied shirt, revealing a clean puncture wound just below his ribs.

"Oh, fuck," I muttered under my breath. The phone at my ear continued to ring until Carlie's voicemail grabbed the call. "Carlie, you need to pick up." I didn't recognize my own voice, which came out sounding like a growl. "I don't have time to explain, but I think someone might be coming after you. Please call me back. Please." I slammed the phone shut before flipping it back open and dialing 911.

I placed Isaac's shirt back down over the wound and pressed down. Isaac screamed, arching his back and kicking his legs in pain as the line rang endlessly. "Goddamn it!"

"I'm sorry. Please don't move." Afraid to wait any longer, I glanced back to Jaime's lifeless body. "Hold this here. Tightly." I placed Isaac's hand over his wound and scrambled to Jaime, fumbling blindly in his pockets for another phone. My search quickly proved fruitful, producing a small, black smartphone. I clicked the lock button and the screen came to life. As it did, I swore my heart stopped beating as the screensaver lit up. A guttural groan from Isaac snapped me back to reality, and I frantically tapped at the emergency call button with slick, bloodied fingers as I crawled back to his side. The line rang for what again felt like ages. As an operator finally picked up, I explained our situation to the best of my ability, which was greatly altered by panic. I looked up at Isaac's face, which had drained of color. His eyelids had become heavy, fluttering unevenly as he fought to stay awake. "Isaac…Isaac." I freed one hand and shook him lightly by the shoulder. "You have to stay awake. Tell me about your mom."

Isaac smiled weakly. His eyes no longer opening. "God, she's the best. I can't wait to see her. She's waiting for me." Isaac's head dropped, his chin hitting his chest and causing his head to loll to the side.

"She's not, Isaac. You're not thinking straight. You need to stay here." Anger bubbled up inside me as I tried in vain to wake him. I barely noticed the minutes passing or the flashing lights approaching us. "You can't do this!" I howled, barely registering the inhuman sounds coming from my body. Tears spilled down my cheeks as I sobbed and screeched, pleading with Isaac to hold on; to say something.

He was silent.

14

Five things I can see. There were thirty-seven white tiles on the floor of the tiny 'pod' that Abby and a nurse had placed me in while they spoke. Two plastic and vinyl chairs rested against the sterile, white wall and an equally plastic recliner occupied the space beneath me in the corner. An untouched bottle of water sat lonely on the floor in front of my feet, the bright fluorescent lights shining on the liquid's surface. A dark rosewood crucifix hung on the wall above the doorframe, keeping a watchful eye on the room.

Four things I can touch. My clothes had become stiff and tacky, Isaac's blood drying quickly in the fabric. My eyes were puffy and sore, and I held an ice pack to the back of my head, where a tender goose egg had already formed. It throbbed with my heartbeat, which kept a galloping pace as I waited for someone, anyone, to give me an update. A second nurse had brought me a blanket, and I pulled it tightly around my bare shoulders as the temperature seemed to drop further and further toward freezing.

Three things I can hear. I listened to the bustle and racket of the Emergency Department just outside my door. Gurney wheels whined and clacked against the vinyl flooring in the hall. The beeping of monitors in the distance reminded me of Isaac's alarm clock. At four-forty-five each morning, he'd wake to a sped up version of the endless electronic ringing that echoed throughout the apartment. I would grumble and roll over on the couch, covering my ears until he hit snooze and I could go back to sleep. I hadn't had a nightmare since the night of the break in, and I had come to understand why so many people talked about naps and sleeping so favorably. Restful sleep was wonderful. I wrestled myself back to the present. *One more... The clock.* A plain, white clock ticked away on the wall across from me. I watched as the second hand clicked forward reliably, forcing the minute hand onward to mark the endless waiting.

Two things I can smell. The sharp, antiseptic scent of cleaning products permeated throughout the halls and was especially strong in my room, which someone had cleaned just as I arrived. It was undercut by the metallic smell of the blood that covered my clothing and skin. The odor had improved over time as the fluid dried, but remained and served as a constant reminder of the night's events.

One thing I can taste. My mouth was dry, my lips cracking painfully and my tongue sticking to my molars. I leaned over to grab my water bottle from the floor. Blue Arctic. It was the same brand I had bought when I first arrived back in Iowa; that Isaac and I had drank at the house when he stopped by to welcome me. I unscrewed the cap and took a hesitant sip. The slightly bitter taste of room temperature bottled water crept along the sides of my tongue, but the liquid eased some of the dryness and cooled my throat.

A knock at the door startled me and I jumped, water sloshing from the bottle and into my lap. Abby entered, a grim expression settled on her face. As much as I didn't think my heart could drop any further, it did. Abby crossed the room to the empty chair next to mine. "May I?"

I nodded, waiting with bated breath as she sat down, leaning forward and resting her elbows on her knees. Abby clasped her hands together and pursed her lips, glancing down to the floor before looking back up at me. "We got him. Dennis is in custody out in Tennessee. He's talking, too."

Relief washed over me as Abby detailed everything that Dennis had confessed regarding his ties to my mother and the money she supposedly owed to him. The relief, however, was temporary as Carlie's face flashed across my mind. "What about my sister?"

Abby sighed heavily, pausing a moment before slowly shaking her head. "He had already gotten to her." I buried my face in the blanket, pressing it hard into my eyes with my fingers. Abby was silent for a few minutes as I processed, continuing only once I had dropped my hands from my now-reddened eyes. "Clarkesville PD is working on getting ahold of her ex-husband to take guardianship of her son. They haven't had any luck yet."

I chewed on my lip, nodding. "Will you let me know when they've gotten someone to take him?" My eyes burned, dried out from exhaustion, and irritated by my assault on them with the blanket. "And, have they said anything about—"

Another knock at the door interrupted me. A petite, dark-haired nurse stood in the doorway. "Am I interrupting?" I piped up immediately to insist that she wasn't, eager with hope that she had news of Isaac. "Okay, well, I have someone who is through surgery, awake, and asking for you quite insistently. I think I've held him off as long as I can at this point. I'm a bit concerned that if I don't get you up there, he'll come down here himself."

My jaw fell in amazement and another surge of relief. "He's okay?"

The nurse smiled. "He's okay." She turned slightly toward the hallway, pointing out with her thumb. "Should we go see him?"

I was out of my chair before she finished the question. "Yes, please," I squeaked, following her out. She led me down a maze of hallways on three different floors, all coded in different color schemes. Stratset was a fairly small city with fairly small businesses, and Pine Valley Hospital was no exception. However, as we continued to weave further and further into the building, I wondered how I would get back outside. I pulled the blanket tighter around my shoulders as we walked, butterflies fluttering wildly in my stomach.

Finally, the nurse stopped. I nearly rear-ended her, so determined to make the journey quickly that I'd gone into autopilot. I came to a stop behind her and watched as she knocked on the door.

"Yeah." His voice.

I closed my eyes as the butterflies became more aggressive, quickening their pace to ram themselves against my ribs. The nurse entered, gesturing for me to follow, and I did. I sucked in a deep, steadying breath as I stepped into the room.

Isaac's face lit up when his eyes met mine. Intense warmth flooded through my chest as my butterflies disintegrated, true relief replacing them.

He looked terrible, though I suspected I didn't look great either. Dark circles surrounded his usually bright eyes, and much of the color had yet to return to his face, save for a large purple bruise along his jawline and a smaller, lighter one on his lower lip. Minor scratches and bruises riddled what I could see of his arms. I hadn't noticed them before, when I'd been so focused on keeping blood in his body. Gauze and stretch-bandage encased his left arm from hand to elbow, his fingers on that hand swollen and discolored. An oxygen tube rested around his neck, likely where it had landed after the last time the nurse put it in his nose. An IV pole stood next to the bed, complete with an obnoxiously beeping pump. Two bags hung from the top, one clear fluid, one blood, connected to Isaac's right hand.

"It's not that bad. C'mere." Isaac smiled. Despite everything, still he smiled.

Isaac patted the bed beside him, and I approached hesitantly, sitting down gingerly at the very edge. He reached out and pulled me to him, holding on to the back of my neck as he hugged me.

"Jesus, Isaac. Be careful. Don't hurt yourself more." My voice struggled against my teeth, which were locked together under the pressure of my chin squeezed to his shoulder.

He let me go, and I sat up. "Sorry. I was just a little worried." Tears welled up in his eyes as he studied me up and down. They glimmered under the lights above. "Are you okay?"

I nodded. "They got Dennis." I looked down at my hands in my lap. Dried blood had caked underneath my fingernails and I picked at it as I continued. "He killed Carlie," I choked. Tears now pricked at my own eyes and I blinked them back.

"Oh god. Why? Did he say anything?" Isaac asked.

"He said everything." I shifted, facing him. "He wanted us all dead. Apparently, he's been making and selling meth in the area for going on thirty years. I don't know how they met, but he said my mom was hiding some of his money for him." Isaac listened intently, patiently waiting as I stopped several times to collect myself. "In our house, of all places! She either actually did, or he thinks she did, take some of the money he stashed. So he followed us to Colorado and tampered with her car. Crazy fuck." I dropped my face into my hands, still failing to wrap my head around all that Dennis had said. "I was supposed to die with her."

Isaac was quiet for a few moments. "Do you think she really did it? Or do you think he was just out of his mind?"

I sat back up. "I don't want to think she did, but I guess I don't know any more. I mean, the money was there, in the house. And the letters?" I clasped my hands behind my neck, stretching, thinking. "And my dad knew something. I don't know what, or how much, but enough to take us and run." I dropped my hands abruptly, my eyes widening. "The trips."

Isaac tilted his head? "What?"

"All those trips she took me on. Mom was a teacher's aide. There's no way Dad gave her money to take just me, and there's no way she could have afforded that shit herself. Oh my god, I'm an idiot." The tears that had threatened me earlier returned with a vengeance, spilling over as I absorbed the idea that my mother had indeed been the reason for my life's lonely path so far. However, she had been the cause of my pain rather than just the biggest missing piece of me.

"You're not. You were a kid." Isaac's jaw set, and I could tell he was upset.

I didn't respond. Carlie had been right. I had pushed away my only remaining family in favor of someone who had left me behind, had put me in danger time and time again. Someone who had gotten herself and Carlie killed and had left two children without their mothers in the name of love for me. I looked back down at my lap. My hands had found their way back together, two of my fingers now bleeding against the nail of another. A tear fell, mixing with the blood and rolling onto my pants.

Isaac spoke again after a few moments. "Did they tell you why Jaime was involved?"

My gaze snapped to meet his. "No, but I think I know why. I'm fairly certain Jaimie's mom, 'Nettie' is Jeanette Goodman. She was with her husband the night he tried to break into a house in Tennessee right around the time our neighbor shot a female intruder. I really shouldn't be telling you all this, but she was in the hospital where I used to work and the first time I met her she kept screaming at me that I would die, calling me all kinds of names. There's no way it's someone else, right? Or am I nuts?"

Isaac was quiet for a while before he responded. "You're right." He took in a deep breath that hitched as he winced in pain. I placed a hand on his knee instinctively. "Jeanette is Nettie, Jaime's mom. Dennis had been using her as a pawn to get Jaime to do his bidding. To get to you. Through me." His eyes grew more distant as he finished the statement, and I lifted a hand to his cheek.

"Isaac, this isn't your fault. Please know that."

Isaac shook his head, grounding himself back in the present. "No, I know. I know. I promise." He forced a small smile, which I returned.

"I'm sorry, honey." I wiped my eyes in a rush and turned around. The nurse had returned, this time with Abby. "We're closing down the floor for the night. Officer Edwards can get you home."

I nodded, standing as Isaac reached into the bedside table. He grabbed my hand, pressing his keys into my palm, but looking at Abby. "Take her to my place. You might want to grab her car, though." He turned to me. "We'll handle the house later, together. Go get a shower and some sleep, and love on Sasha a bit. I'll be outta here before we know it." He squeezed my hand and smiled before letting me go. I walked to the door, where Abby and the nurse no longer stood. They had stepped into the hallway, waiting for me. Isaac called after me as I approached the exit. "Hey!"

I turned back. "Hm?"

"Will you stay? Around, I mean." His smile had left his face, leaving his expression serious.

I smirked. He wanted me to stay? I didn't think I could leave him if I tried. I whirled around, marching back over to him. He opened his mouth to speak but I stopped him, planting a hard kiss on his lips. "Maybe for a while." All my cards now on the table, I studied Isaac's expression, our faces still just inches apart. His eyes were wide, locked on mine. He dropped his jaw in shock, but the corners of his mouth curved upward in a smile as his face turned a vibrant shade of red. He exhaled a chuckle and closed his mouth, nodding. I turned again for the door, beaming as I crossed the threshold.

EPILOGUE

Six months later – Coalwick

I had been walking for several minutes, lost. When I finally found the right place, I dropped to the ground and sat cross-legged in the lush grass. "This feels crazy; talking to you like you can hear me." My hands shook, the paper clutched in my fingers rattling. I wiped each of my palms on my pants one by one. *Why am I anxious right now?* "I'm seeing someone to talk to. Therapy, I guess. This letter is my homework for the week. I have one for Dad and Carlie too, that I would read to them if they were closer."

Mom's headstone sat silently in front of me. I could see a blurry version of myself in the glassy black granite. I looked around me. Lily Vale Memorial Park was peaceful and colorful. Vibrant flowers dotted the grass, tokens of remembrance for hundreds of loved ones lost to the earth. Just beyond the wrought-iron fence at the back of the lot, a field of white daisies basked in the summer sunlight. I smiled, taking in the scenery as a warm breeze floated across the ground. I was glad that Mom had been resting in such a beautiful place, though this was my first visit.

Looking back at the letter in my hands, I started reading. "I miss you. It has taken me a while, but I forgive you. I still don't understand exactly why you did what you did, but I would rather have you here with me still… It doesn't matter anymore. I'm doing a lot better. I have a job now, at Pat's. And I live upstairs in the next building over, above the pharmacy. In a few months, I'm hoping I'll have enough saved to go back to school."

I glanced over my shoulder as an older couple walked by. I took a breath, calming the embarrassment that rose in my gut. "I'm not keeping the house. We went through most of the stuff and I kept a few things, but the rest is still there."

I stopped. *We*. My thoughts raced, fumbling out of my mouth on top of each other. "I didn't add this to the letter, because my therapist said it should be about me. But I'm taking a sidebar quick. And this is kind of about me. I'm not alone anymore. It's been like six months, and I still can't believe it, but I met someone that has made this move back so much easier. His name is Isaac, and Mom, you would have loved him." I checked behind me again to ensure the coast was clear. "I'm starting to think I do." I laughed, a bubbly, joyful sound I had heard more often in the time I had been back home than in all the years I spent in Tennessee. I had missed really laughing.

Deciding that I'd had enough, I folded the paper back up. Searching the surrounding ground, I found a stone. I used it to weigh the letter down, leaving it in the grass in front of the headstone as I stood. I dusted the grass off of my jeans and kissed my fingertips before tapping them on the top of the headstone. "I love you."

Feeling lighter, I weaved through several rows of graves to get back to the gravel pathway. I walked for a little while, taking time to read some of the stones as I passed. Finally, I reached the edge of the cemetery, where Isaac's new truck waited for me. A bright white, the massive vehicle was a big change from his last one. I shaded my eyes from the sun with a hand as I approached. Isaac rolled the window down and I smirked at him. "Nice ride." I opened the door and hoisted myself into the passenger seat.

Isaac's face reddened. "You don't have to say that every time you see it anymore." We laughed as I fastened my seatbelt and Isaac pulled toward the cemetery gates.

I grinned. "What fun would it be if I stopped now? You gotta get some dirt on it first, then I'll quit."

"Fine." He smiled back at me, resting his left hand on top of the wheel as he drove. A short, fat scar stood out against his now deeply tanned skin at the base of his hand. He caught me looking and held his arm up. "We match now."

"That's kinda what I was thinking, too." I looked at my own wrist, expecting to feel the same familiar shame I had always felt. Instead, I thought of Isaac's scar, and Isaac himself. All the memories we had shared in such a short time flooded me with gratitude. Without him, I would likely still be at the house, sifting through old shit and staring at a months-late U-Haul rental in the overgrown yard.

Green cornstalks raced by in a blur as we neared the house. I watched as they slowed, their outlines becoming clearer as Isaac braked, pulling into a field entrance across the road from the house. The bed of the truck lined up neatly with the front door, which sat ajar. A huge red fire engine idled in the driveway, firefighters trudging around the yard with hoses and other equipment as Isaac and I got out of the truck. We moved to the truck bed, and Isaac had to lift me up to sit on the tailgate. He hopped up after me with some difficulty. "Too tall for ya?" I teased.

He shot me a look. "Hop down and get back up here yourself, short stuff."

I feigned offense, which was short-lived as I burst into giggles. "Fair enough. I'm on the tall side for women, though. Don't forget it."

Isaac laughed and scooted backward, settling himself on the warm metal. He rested a hand on my thigh. "You ready for this?" He watched my expression carefully as I considered the question.

I put my hand on top of his. "Yes. Very." I smiled, watching the scene unfolding across from us as Isaac patted my leg in response. The sunlight faded as one of the firefighters entered the house. A few minutes passed, and I jumped, pointing out a small billow of smoke that had started to leak out of the upstairs window. My bedroom window. The Stratset Fire Department had removed all the power lines from the house and had cut the overgrown trees back to a safe distance. They had jumped at the opportunity to do live burn training, and I was happy to offer it. "I can't believe we got to do this." I watched in awe as the firefighter re-emerged from the front door, turning to watch the smoke thicken and darken.

I moved closer to Isaac, resting my head on his shoulder as flames licked the windowpane and spread rapidly. Isaac put his arm around me, and I welcomed the warmth of his skin as the sun disappeared behind the trees. He traced up and down on my arm with his thumb as the fire engulfed the entire house.

More units had shown up as time had gone on, and finally someone shouted, "Water, go!" Every person jumped into action to extinguish the flames. It was amazing to witness. We watched the burn for more than an hour, the intense heat radiating all the way to us and beyond.

As the blaze died down, I felt Isaac rest his head on top of mine, planting a kiss on top of my head. I beamed, my face heating even more. "Should we go? We can stay if you want."

I replied quickly. "No. I'm ready to go. They're probably about done, anyway." I sat up straight, stretching my back out before sliding off the truck bed to the ground. Isaac followed suit and closed the tailgate.

We took our places back in the truck, and Isaac backed out onto the road. As we drove away, I watched my past fade away on the right, and my future, still smiling, on the left.

www.ingramcontent.com/pod-product-compliance
Lightning Source LLC
Chambersburg PA
CBHW060332310726

48976CB00007B/2530